HER LAST NEW YEARS EVE

VICTORIA MATTSEN CRIME SERIES
BOOK 10

IFEANYI ESIMAI

eISBN: 978-1-63589-814-9
Print ISBN: 978-1-63589-815-6
Audio ISBN: 978-1-63589-816-3
Cover design by coveredbymelinda.com

Published by ShotReads, an imprint of
Ciparum LLC
270 Sparta Ave., Suite 104, PMB 152
Sparta, NJ 07871

Get a FREE copy of The Rookie!

Join my Newsletter for updates, giveaways, teasers, and a FREE copy of the prequel - The Rookie. Click here or scan the QR code.

For Chinwe...Always.
The wind beneath my wings.

ACKNOWLEDGMENTS

My heartfelt gratitude goes out to my family and friends, whose unwavering faith in me fueled this project from the very start.

I also want to extend a special thanks to a group of incredible individuals whose generous spirit has made an indelible impact on this project, and for that, I am forever grateful.

Erik S
Nneka Anaebonam
Craig Martelle
Jenn Davidson
Chinwe Anyamele
Obioha Emezie
Renee
Okechukwu Obua
Romeo Richards
Ikenna Emeghara
Charles Onunkwo
Adaeze

Every one of you has helped shape this journey in your own unique way, and I couldn't be more thankful. Your support has not only made these books a reality but has also inspired me as I continue to tell Detective Vikki Mattsen's story.

To all the readers, thank you for inviting Detective Vikki

Mattsen into your lives. It's been a joy to share this adventure with you.

Here's to the stories yet to be told.

PROLOGUE

Alexis cocked her head. Was that the doorbell? She'd come out of the shower minutes earlier. Dressed in her satin-green pajamas, she sat in front of her dressing mirror, putting finishing touches on her face as per her nightly skincare ritual. She and Vikki had barely talked at the St. Patrick's Day donation dinner before her father had whisked Vikki away—to take care of family business, he'd said.

The doorbell chimed again. Who could it be at this time of the night? A thought occurred to her. She sprang to her feet and grabbed her housecoat. She'd better get it before her father did.

Her dad was coming out of his room. "Are you going to get that?"

"Yep. It must be Vikki. Maybe she forgot her key. I can't wait to hear all about Paris." She swept past him. "You seem tired, more like sad. Didn't you get enough donations?"

Before her dad could reply, she was on the stairs. She took them two at a time, leaped off the last step, and crossed the foyer. She glanced at the grandfather clock standing like a sentry next to the statue of Venus. The time was a few minutes before midnight.

A dark silhouette about Vikki's height stood on the other side of the frosted glass door. A smile tugged at the corner of Alexis' lips. Chest heaving from the mad rush down, she turned the lock and pulled the door open. The smell of stale beer and sweat rushed in.

The smile vanished from her face. A cold chill traveled down her spine. It was the guy from the bar. He'd tried to buy her a drink, and she'd politely refused. *He followed me home.*

Alexi swallowed. "What do you want?"

"Hi, do you remember me?" The man's voice was slurred and gravelly. "We met at Dave's bar. We have unfinished business."

This was bad news. "Why don't you come back tomorrow when you're sober." Alexis started to close the door.

He stuck a foot in. "Not so fast." He licked his lips, his gaze traveling from Alexis' face to her chest.

Alexis didn't need to glance down to know her housecoat was open. She let go of the door and wrapped the coat around her body, her second mistake of the night. The first had been assuming it was Vikki.

That was all the man needed. He shoved her back. He was in.

"Get out! Or I'll call the police!" Her voice shook with rage and fear.

He leaned back on the door, and it clicked shut. He glanced around. "Wow...this crib is sick!"

"Get out!" This was one of those rare times when she didn't have her phone with her. She couldn't go back upstairs to get it and call the cops.

"Look at the titties on that babe." He staggered to the statue of Venus de Milo and ran his hand over her breasts.

Alexis secured her coat with the belt. She grabbed the

man by the elbow and pulled him toward the door. With her other hand, she turned the knob.

"Hey...I'm not ready to go yet."

Alexis tugged too hard. The man hurtled into her and slammed her against the door.

"You want to play? I-I bet you're softer than that piece of stone."

Rough hands landed on her chest and squeezed. She wanted to scream, but fear clamped her mouth shut. He wrapped his hands around her waist and lifted her. He staggard backward into the half table in the foyer.

"Hey! Let her go now!" a voice thundered.

Alexis' eyes shot up. Her father stood at the top of the stairs with a pistol pointed at them.

He walked down to the staircase landing. "Let her go, now!"

The man pulled Alexis tighter against him.

"Y-you are not going to shoot. You might hit her. I-I have a gun, too, you know." He belched.

The smell was nauseating. Alexis' dinner crawled up her throat like beer foam in a glass. She swallowed.

Her father raised his other hand. He had a phone.

The man fumbled around his waistband. A pistol suddenly appeared, raised and pointed at Alexis' father. His hand trembled like a flag in a hurricane. The gun barked once. The force of the recoil pushed him back. His grasp on Alexis tightened.

Alexis' heart raced. A deafening ringing filled her ears. She couldn't move, couldn't speak, couldn't even cry out. All she could do was stare in disbelief. Her father tumbled down the stairs and crumpled on the floor.

"Oh my god, I got him," the man said.

Alexis' body trembled. She felt like she was hovering above, watching her father gasping for air. She must get to him. Call an ambulance. Alexis jerked her head back and heard a sickening crunch.

The man let her go. "My nose!"

She ran to him, and got on her knees. His shirt was soaked with blood. "D-Daddy. Oh—" Something hard slammed into the side of her face. Light flashed around her. Pain exploded in her head, and she went down.

"Bitch! You broke my nose!"

Alexis was on her back. The voice sounded far away. A shadow loomed over her. Alexis felt a hand around her neck, and it squeezed. She reached for it to get it off, but it got tighter. Darkness crawled in from the corner of her eyes. She struggled, tried to draw in air, then everything went dark.

CHAPTER ONE

Vikki sat up. The open file on her lap slipped off her bare thigh onto the bed. She tugged the oversized tee shirt over her leg. It didn't go far. She'd finished reading the case file from Ashton Township in Long Island for the murders of Alexis and Mike Devoe. It had arrived a day before Christmas.

She turned off the reading lamp on the nightstand and glanced at the digital clock. It was eleven-fifteen p.m.

Light streamed in from a lamp in the parking lot. Christmas had come and gone, but its fingerprints still lingered—the smells of cinnamon and apple cider from a candle burned earlier hung in the air. Outside the window, snowflakes came down like chopped-up bird feathers floating perpetually as if Santa was still on his way.

Vikki hugged her legs, her chin resting on her head. She watched Ted sleep. He looked so peaceful.

Even though he was beside her, Vikki felt their relationship had been strained for the past few weeks without any conflict. Or maybe it was only her. Two months ago, she'd have gotten hot and bothered watching him. But now, she felt empty inside.

Vikki thought she'd overcome her past, but it seemed to have become a permanent fixture. Despite Ted hanging in there, refusing to be pushed away, and she falling for him, she still felt responsible for what had happened to Bruce.

Bruce had been her training officer and boyfriend and was ready to propose to her the day he'd got shot. They were on a routine foot patrol, and she'd noticed an altercation between two couples. She wished she hadn't gone back.

She'd given Ted a train set for Christmas. The boyish enthusiasm he'd exuded made her heart thud like an African talking drum.

Despite warning him not to get her anything, he had. She'd been mad when he'd presented her with a gift. A beautiful scarf she'd tried on once at the mall. She'd wrapped it around her neck and struck a few poses in front of the mirror. It was soft and silky, with delicate florals and swirling paisleys in a burst of bright colors. Vikki had planned to buy it later, but Ted had been paying attention. She'd kissed him and forgotten about not wanting anything in the first place.

They'd celebrated Christmas at his apartment, enjoyed a quiet dinner, and only when they'd returned to her place to get a change of clothes had she seen the envelope addressed to her.

Vikki had seen the return address and knew where it came from. She'd contemplated not opening it until later in the new year, but curiosity had got the better of her.

A shiver shot through her. Reading what the investigators thought had happened made her angry. The killer had shot Mike and strangled Alexis. The murder weapon was not recovered, and the ballistics on the bullet didn't match any in their database.

Vikki's vision was cloudy from unshed tears. She remembered the first time she and Alexis had met. She was hospital-ized, recuperating from her wounds after an explosion at their trailer. She'd escaped with minor cuts and a ringing in her ear. Alexis' father, a physician at the hospital, had come in one Sunday with his family on their way back from church. He and his wife had found Alexis in the reception area talking to a girl when it was time to go.

Vikki had wandered out of the ward and ended up in the hospital's lobby. She must have fallen asleep because she'd woken with a start. She'd been nudged.

A girl about her age—blonde, piercing blue eyes—had smiled at her. She'd reached for Vikki's face with a tissue, and Vikki had jerked back.

"You have drool on your mouth," the girl said. "I do that, too, when I sleep."

Vikki stared at her.

"I'm Alexis, Alexis Devoe. What's your name?" She extended the Kleenex to Vikki.

Vikki took it and wiped the corner of her mouth and under her chin. It was like she'd been spitting on herself while she slept. She glanced at the girl with round blue eyes, dressed in a flowery sundress, and looked away. She remembered her manners. "Thank you. I-I'm Victoria, Vikki Mattsen."

They didn't say much. They sat and watched TV together. About ten minutes later, a woman, a larger version of Alexis, came to them.

"Alex is your dad out yet?" the woman said.

Alexis shook her head. "Mommy, this is my friend, Vikki."

The woman smiled. "Pleased to meet you, Vikki. I'm Sandy." She shook Vikki's hand. Her gaze lingered on her. She must have noticed her hospital gown and scanned the reception area, looking tense. A man waved at her. Her features relaxed, and she smiled.

The man in a blue button-down shirt and chino pants motioned to them in a 'let's go' signal.

Alexis' mother smiled. "Nice meeting you, Vikki. Come on, Alex."

Vikki watched the woman walk to him. He slipped his hand around her waist, pulled her closer, and pecked her on each cheek. They turned in her direction.

The long and short of it was that Alexis refused to move until she was assured Vikki was coming home with them. A perplexed Dr. Devoe spoke to Vikki. They took her back to her floor and learned about her situation from the nurse.

"She lost both parents in an explosion and fire accident," the nurse said, shaking her head. "So far, no relative has been located. The social worker is considering finding a family for her. The foster care system is a double-edged sword."

Alexis had been carried home kicking and screaming. Dr. and Mrs. Devoe were put in a situation they couldn't walk away from with their conscience intact. The girl was an orphan, and their daughter had taken a liking to her.

They began the process of becoming foster parents. Vikki was discharged from the hospital to a group home. Only later did she learn what the Devoes had to endure to become her foster parents. Endless interviews, testing, classroom training, background checks—even Alexis was interviewed. It took almost twelve months before everything was in place.

Within a week after they'd got their license, Vikki moved in with them. The Devoes treated her like their daughter, and she was always on her best behavior. When Alexis' mother was snatched away from them by ovarian cancer, Vikki shared their pain.

Ted moved, breaking his rhythmic breathing, and pulled Vikki out of her reminiscing.

Vikki refocused on the file, imagining what Alexis must have gone through at the hands of the killer to suffer those injuries. Her cause of death had been ruled as asphyxiation by strangulation. Her dad had been shot straight in the heart.

Vikki's whole body shook. Her phone buzzed. She took a deep breath, exhaled, and picked it up. It was a reminder. It was the twenty-eighth of December. The text said: *Happy Birthday, Alexis.*

Vikki felt like a fist had pierced her chest, grabbed her heart, and squeezed. She gasped for air. A whimper escaped her throat, and the floodgates opened. She sobbed, her body racked by bottled-up emotions.

Ted stirred, then turned over and lay on his back.

Vikki wiped her tears with the back of her hand. He shouldn't see her like this.

CHAPTER TWO

Vikki hadn't planned on waking Ted. But it was too late. He raised his head and reached for her.

"Babe, what's wrong?"

Vikki stilled herself.

He ran his hands over her shoulder and squeezed. He must have felt something because he sat up and started with deep tissue massages.

"You're wound up like a cobra. Bad dream?"

Vikki's tense muscles began to relax. She welcomed the contact, but she refused to speak. If she tried, she'd turn into a blabbering mess.

Ted ran his hands up and down her arm, whispering soothing words. He stopped and leaned forward. "Oh no, you read the case file?" He exhaled and held her tighter. "I'm so sorry. You shouldn't have. At least not at night."

Vikki rested her head on his shoulder and said nothing. She inhaled, filling her lungs as far as possible, then let it out slowly. It seemed to calm her. She knew what he was thinking —she was too close to the case. There was no doubt about that.

Ted resumed kneading her muscles. "Babe, you're too close to the case." His voice was gentle and nonjudgmental. "It happens to everyone, even doctors. Every autopsy seems like another day at the office until you pull back the sheet and it's someone you knew. I can't imagine what you're going through now." He sighed. "You've read the file—there's no unreading it. Can you put it aside, and we'll try and make the best of what's left of the holiday?"

She knew he was on her side but wanted to scream *no*. "I know their killer is out there in Long Island…I can feel it." Vikki never had a sister, and Alexis had stuck to her more than any sister could have. And some bastard had snuffed out her life. Vikki's breathing came faster as her anger renewed.

Ted must have sensed it, too. He resumed his massage of her shoulder.

"In the new year, we'll both take time off and go to New York," Ted said. "See what we can find out, as planned."

Vikki couldn't understand why it had taken her this long to try and find out what had happened to her family. Granted, there had been delays in getting the file to her, but over the years, she hadn't been compelled enough—she felt sick to her stomach.

"There's a time for everything," Ted said.

Vikki nodded. The words went in one ear and came out the other. She resumed her thoughts. She couldn't let the killer continue to breathe. She should have gone after whoever it was right after it had happened. Then she reminded herself that she'd been fresh out of college, had no skills, and didn't even know who could have done it. The same reasons that had stopped her from searching for who'd done it ten years ago had convinced her to join the police. Get the training and then dive in.

She refocused on what Ted was saying.

"Remember, you don't have any jurisdiction there. We can get them to reopen the case—"

Vikki interrupted him. "But it took them so long to send the case file even after the request was approved. I don't see how they'll be eager to reopen a case."

Ted nodded. He was silent for a moment. "I still have my PI license. It's good for Minnesota, New York, and New Jersey. I could snoop around come January."

Vikki had forgotten about that. "That could work, but I don't want to wait that long."

"January is next week."

"I've waited too long already," Vikki protested. "Do you know what today is?"

Ted pursed his lips. "No." He smiled. "The thirtieth?"

"Yes." Vikki raised her phone and tapped the screen with a finger. "But also Alexis' birthday. I'd set a reminder. For the past ten years, I did nothing."

"No, you became a detective. Now you have the skills to do something about it and a plan to make it happen. It will be January first in two more days, and things will return to normal. You can't investigate a crime when everybody is still on holiday." He squeezed her. "I need the bathroom. I'll be right back."

"Okay."

He took the covers off and stared at his red pajama bottoms with surprise. It wasn't his style. "I forgot we were matching." He headed for the bathroom.

Ted returned five minutes later.

"Did I ever tell you how Alexis and I met?" Vikki asked.

He shook his head.

She snuggled close to him. "She saved my life. I'd have probably ended up in a group home or foster home. Perhaps dead by now." She told him about going to the hospital after a gas explosion had killed her mother and stepfather. How Alexis had seen her taking a nap in the reception area, and they'd become fast friends.

"No wonder you feel the way you do," Ted said. "She was an angel walking the earth."

Vikki smiled. She liked that. But she hadn't told him the whole story. The shame was still there despite how long it had been. Vikki's mother had perfected the art of picking losers. First was Vikki's biological dad, a drunk and drug user. He'd beaten her mother up at the slightest provocation. When Vikki had gone to her mother's rescue, he'd use her as a punching bag, then put her in the kitchen cabinet where he'd kept his liquor.

A shiver ran down her spine as she remembered.

Ted draped the blanket over her shoulders. "Better?"

Vikki nodded. Her mind drifted back to her childhood. She was in a cramped, dark closet with her knees pressed tight against her chest, inhaling alcohol fumes until she was woozy. She'd hear her mother's cries as her drunk father beat her, then took her by force.

When things quietened, he'd open the cabinet and grab a bottle of whiskey. When that was done, his groping hands pulled Vikki out, and she got the same treatment as her mother. No, she wasn't going to share that with Ted. Some secrets were meant to be taken to the grave.

The desire to take matters into her own hands and find justice for Alexis and her father was rekindled with a feverish passion. "I want to start today. Travel to New York and see what I can do."

Ted drew in a deep breath and exhaled noisily. "Are you sure? The new year is days away. Right now, my schedule is free, and yours isn't. You'll be AWOL."

"I feel the urge now. By the new year, it might pass—same

as in previous years." Vikki was quiet for a moment. "When... when she saw me in that hospital lobby, she didn't hesitate to help me. The least I can do is find justice for them."

Ted drew her closer. "Let's get some sleep. We'll leave in the morning."

CHAPTER THREE

Ted had been called in early in the morning following a traffic accident with fatalities. Alcohol intoxication was thought to have played a part in the collision. Injuries, tests, and causes of death needed to be determined and documented. One of the vehicles had been traveling in the opposite direction on a highway exit ramp.

Vikki waited for Ted to finish. Two good heads were always better than one, but when another fatality presented as soon as he'd wrapped up the first one, she had no choice but to leave without him.

"I'll come and join you as soon as this is done," Ted said.

She'd started the car, turned on the heat, and let the engine run. Vikki entered the vehicle ten minutes later. It was toasty and had a faint smell of burned plastic. Her black puffer-down jacket over a blue sweater and jeans now seemed too much. She turned the heat down, removed her coat, and laid it on the backseat.

She stopped at a gas station and filled the tank of her dependable white Ford Explorer. She bought a cup of coffee and was on her way. Joining I-80 E around four-ten p.m. was no hassle. Despite the heavy snowfall last night, the roads were clear. St. Ives Township was putting her tax money to excellent use.

She drove with her radio off, exhausted from Christmas jingles on the radio. This year they had started before Thanksgiving. Every year they started earlier and earlier.

Vikki pressed down on the pedal with her ankle-length tan suede boot, and the car lunged forward. She wished she'd changed into her Crocs. It'd be more comfortable for an hour-plus drive. As long as they didn't run into a Bridgegate-like situation, she'd survive wearing the boots. She shuddered, wondering how the people stuck on the bridge peed and took care of number two.

In 2013, aides to the then-governor of New Jersey allegedly conspired to close lanes, resulting in people spending four hours on the bridge on their commutes instead of the usual thirty minutes.

Vikki was about ten minutes into the trip when her phone showed an incoming call. It was her friend, Angie. She answered it. "Girl reporter!"

"Merry Christmas and a happy New Year!"

"Where are you now? Visiting another European country?"

"I'm in Germany with Thomas."

Vikki laughed. "You sound thrilled."

"I am. Thomas is fantastic! We should do this together next Christmas holiday. You bring Ted with you. What are you up to?"

A good idea, Vikki thought. "On my way to New York. Something came up."

"Don't tell me you're working. You better be going there to watch the ball drop at Times Square for the New Year count—"

Angie cut off as if someone was talking to her.

"Vikki, I have to go. My man calls. Extend my regards to Ted and Gomez. Miss you. Bye!" The line went dead.

Vikki had a smile on her face when the GPS said, "Stay on the left lane for George Washington Bridge." She hoped there wouldn't be a Bridgegate.

She was happy Thomas had swept Angie off her feet. They'd met when she'd gone to Atlanta. Angie said it was love at first sight. Vikki smiled. She'd had one of those before. That was Ted. Bruce had been more like enemies to lovers. The smile faded as she wondered what the new year might bring for her and Ted. This was the longest she'd ever been with anyone since Bruce had died. Deep down, she still blamed herself.

Ted once told her that people left behind had a running monologue, second-guessing themselves, trying to figure out what they could have done better to prevent or stop what had happened.

Was justice possible from this trip to New York? Should she have waited for the new year before launching her investigation to at least have more resources? And remain on Captain Levin's good side?

Traffic slowed as she got closer to the toll booth at Fort Lee. Beyond that was the George Washington Bridge. Vikki switched to the left EZ pass lane and stayed there. She wasn't a fan of changing lanes. From her experience, it was like exchanging one set of problems for another.

Traffic on the bridge wasn't bad. It was moving at a steady clip. Maybe it was because of the time of the year. The magnificent brown Hudson River shimmered in the fading sunlight to her left and right.

People strolled, jogged, and cycled along the cage-fenced sidewalk on the bridge, relishing the spectacular view of New York City. Between 2014 and 2016, thirty people committed suicide by jumping off GWB, hence the meshwork.

Vikki's mind drifted to another body of water—smaller, but it had claimed her father's life. An accidental drowning, the police had called it. It happened all the time.

Vikki and her mother had then lived in the trailer. They'd both welcomed the relief. The beatings, abuse, and assaults had stopped. Vikki was no longer placed in the cabinet with the alcohol bottles and yanked out for her father's entertainment. They'd even got money from his life insurance. It was fun times all the way.

At first, her mother had been conservative, spending as little as possible. Then she'd got bolder and hung out to enjoy her newfound freedom and liberation. She'd spent money like it was going out of fashion. She'd rekindled and reinforced old habits and picked up new ones, including prescription drugs and the man who later became Vikki's stepfather.

Nobody was feeding the goose that laid the golden eggs. The bank account gave up its last dollar, and the nightmare returned, this time with a vengeance. What followed was more like changing lanes while driving. They swapped one set of problems for another.

Vikki pushed the thought out of her mind. Soon she'd arrive at the house where she'd lived after her mother and stepfather had died. Those had been the happiest years of her life until that St. Patrick's day.

CHAPTER FOUR

Vikki turned onto Fox Run Street, Ashton, New York, her heart pounding, body tense, coiled tight like a jack-in-the-box about to spring out. It was six p.m., and darkness had crept into her former street.

The homes hadn't changed much. Maybe she was seeing them with new eyes after being away for such a long time. The houses and yards were lit up with blinking colored Christmas lights.

The Christmas decorations were overboard now than when she'd lived there. Her pulse raced the closer she got to the number twenty-three. For some unknown reason, Vikki expected to see Alexis or her father backing out of the driveway.

She passed the house, made a U-turn, and parked in front of the Greek Revival. She wondered if the new owners were home. Two security lamps illuminated the main entrance door. One hung over each door of the three-car garage doors at the side of the building. A pair adorned the gate pillars.

The house was not readied for the celebration of the birth of Christ. No Christmas tree with twinkling decorations close to the window for people to know that Santa was welcomed in the home.

Her eyes drifted to the opposite neighbor's home. A Christmas wreath hung on the door. Two evergreen pine trees near the entrance were illuminated by bright bulbs strewn over them. The snow-covered lawn boasted three lit reindeer in a single file attached to a sleigh. A crude snowman with a carrot sticking out as its nose stood close to the sleigh. Vikki smiled. There were probably children in that home.

Vikki's gaze returned to her former home. They'd moved from the city to Long Island just before she and Alexis had gone to college, and they hadn't known their neighbors.

She and Alexis were age mates, but Vikki had lived a hard life and was like an older sister watching a younger sibling. She was grateful that all the time she'd lived there, there had never been any friction with Alexis, even when they'd had their differences.

Vikki removed the seat belt and got her jacket from the backseat. Her pulse picked up a notch. What was she going to say when they opened the door? *Hello, I'm Detective Mattsen. I'm here to investigate the murder of my family in this house ten years ago. Can I come in?*

Vikki cringed. That was the worst thing to say to anyone during this festive period. What if they didn't know people had died in their home?

Well, she was here already. She should have thought about all that before coming out here. Maybe Ted was right. She should have at least waited for the new year. Thinking of Ted, Vikki sent him a text. She'd arrived and was at the house, about to ring the bell.

Vikki waited a minute. No reply. She decided he was still in the morgue. He'd return her text when he had the time. She killed the engine, opened the door, and stepped out.

The cold air enveloped her. She zipped up her jacket,

slipped her hands into her pockets, and walked up the driveway.

Her mind drifted to this same driveway on March seventeenth, ten years ago. She'd stepped out of the yellow cab. "Keep the change," she'd said to the cab driver.

Luxury cars were parked along the road. Muffled music drifted down to her as she dragged her hand luggage up the driveway. She was tempted to enter the house from the garage and avoid the crowd or whatever was happening, then changed her mind.

She rang the bell, and a uniformed, middle-aged man dressed as a leprechaun opened the door.

"Happy St. Patrick's Day!" said the man, smiling. "I'm Patrick. And you are..."

"Victoria Mattsen. I live here. What's going on?"

"Your sister, Alexis, mentioned you'd be arriving today. It's a fundraiser to raise awareness about cleft lip and palate." The man raised a shoulder and shook his head. "I don't know what that means."

Vikki nodded. She knew about it through Dr. Mike Devoe. It was a common orofacial defect fixed by cheiloplasty. "Ah, I didn't know it'd be held in the house here."

Patrick removed his green hat, bowed, and waved her in.

Vikki wheeled her hand luggage to a corner in the foyer, right beside the marble statue of Venus, the Roman goddess of love. She checked her hair in the mirror over the half table and entered the living room. The center table in the middle of the room had been removed, creating an open space for people to mingle.

Bowler hats perched on some of the men's heads. A few paraded in leprechaun costumes. The women were elegant in green or pinned shamrocks on their gowns. The smell of perfumes, cologne, and food hung in the air. Her stomach rumbled.

"Vikki!" a familiar voice said.

Vikki whirled.

Mike Devoe, hands spread out, wearing a green jacket, walked quickly toward her. They embraced her. He lifted her and swung her around.

"Good to see you. Happy St. Patrick's Day. How was your flight?"

"Good to see you, too. It was excellent."

Mike's glance darted to the guests around him. "My other daughter arrived from Paris."

Heat rose to Vikki's cheeks. She always felt embarrassed whenever Mike referred to her as his daughter. The Devoes had wanted to adopt her, but after her experiences with her biological father and stepfather, she associated being anyone's legal child with abuse. She'd declined, but the Devoes were her legal guardians.

Right then, she wished she hadn't refused to be their daughter. Mike Devoe was the most devoted father figure she'd ever had. Vikki smiled and waved shyly at the visitors.

Vikki's name was yelled out again. This time it was Alexis. Tall, with blue eyes and a shamrock in her blonde hair, she was stunning in her little green dress. They hugged and held each other tight.

"Vikki, come and see me in the study when you can," Mike Devoe said. "I have something for you."

Vikki nodded.

He waved and rejoined his guests.

Vikki and Alexis retreated to a corner and traded stories and experiences about college life in their respective schools. Alexis wanted Vikki to come to a new bar, the Mirage, in the next town.

"I'll take a rain check. I have to babysit some model friends who came with me from Paris. Let's go tomorrow," Vikki said. "I told them I'll return to Manhattan to make sure they'd settled in."

"Tomorrow is good," Alexis said.

Vikki was jolted back to the present as a sudden blast of wind hurled snow into her face. That was the last time she'd seen Alexis and her dad alive.

She rang the bell about four times, and nobody came to the door. No sound came from the house, and no inside lights were on.

Even though the driveway and the walkway to the house were cleared of snow, she'd anticipated nobody was home, but now it was confirmed. She'd come this far. She should at least find out who lived there and maybe peep inside.

Vikki looked around. The curtain on a window in the house across the street moved. Someone was watching her. She knew where to go.

CHAPTER FIVE

Vikki crossed the road and approached the white Cape Cod. Back in the day, it had belonged to an empty nester who was getting ready to relocate to Florida. The snowman and amount of decoration on the home suggested a young family with little children lived there now.

The curtain moved again. She was being watched. Vikki walked to the door. A dog barked. Moments later, footsteps approached. The lock turned, and the door opened a slit.

A woman in her late twenties, with her blonde hair tied in a ponytail, smiled at her. "Hi."

Vikki smiled. She knew they'd been watching her from the window, so she used that to her advantage. "Hello, so sorry to bother you. I was at your neighbor's place across the street and wondered whether they are in town."

The woman gave Vikki a polite smile but said nothing. The gears were turning in her head, searching for something to say.

"I'm sure they don't live here anymore," Vikki said. "I'm talking of close to ten years ago. Sorry to bother you. I'll go."

Before she moved away, she noticed something change in the woman's eyes. Recognition? Sympathy?

"Wait."

Vikki turned.

"The house has been empty since we moved here about seven years ago."

Vikki pointed behind her. "But the driveway...it's...it's clear of snow."

"The lawn is mowed in the spring and summer, too," the woman said, sighing. "You said you're looking for a woman you haven't seen in a decade, and she used to live there?"

Vikki nodded. A white lie. That's what her mother had said after Vikki's father died. Now she was telling her own.

"I think the current owner lives abroad. But ten years ago, I heard a doctor lived there with his two daughters. One night, he and one daughter were murdered by an intruder."

Before Vikki responded, the clatter of claws on the wooden floor was followed by barking and running feet.

"Mommy, our warm air is leaving." The voice belonged to a girl of about six. She stood beside her mother and watched Vikki with interest.

The dog ran out of the door, sniffed at Vikki's boots, and barked. Vikki bent down and scratched its head. It dashed back into the house.

"The dog likes you. Sorry for my manners. I'm Taylor. And this is my daughter, Samantha. Why don't you come in?"

"I'm Victoria. Sorry, I don't want to impose."

"Nonsense. As Samantha said, it's cold out there."

Vikki stepped into the foyer and shut the door behind her. She glanced around and said, "You have a nice house. So you were saying...about the people who lived in the house?"

Before Taylor could respond, a man suddenly emerged—a youthful figure, roughly the same age as Vikki, dressed in a blue V-neck sweater and jeans.

His hair was brown like the little girl's. They had the same upturned shape of the nose.

"This is my husband, John," Taylor said. "Victoria."

"Hi," John said and shook hands with Vikki.

Taylor glanced at her husband. "Vikki was across the street searching for the family that lived there before..." She didn't finish the sentence. "I think her friend is one of the girls."

John's eyes fixed on Vikki. "I'm so sorry. It was such a tragedy. We heard about it after we moved in."

"Sweetie," Taylor said. "What's the story with the current owner? He doesn't live there, right?"

John shrugged. "I think he lives abroad. One of those people who own property as an investment." He smiled. "I'm not complaining. The lawn and the house are well maintained. I don't know the details about the family that lived in the house apart from the tragedy. Maybe you should drop by the Ashton Police Station. There must be someone you can talk to about what happened and maybe get a forwarding address."

Vikki nodded. An awkward silence followed this. She didn't know who owned the house now, but it had been left to her and Alexis in Mike Devoe's will. An orphan with no relatives, he'd split his property between Vikki and Alexis. In his will, Mike Devoe had referred to her as his daughter.

Vikki had refused to be formally adopted and was devastated when his will was read, and she'd inherited that much of his property. With Alexis dead, everything she had went to Vikki. The police had questioned her hard, but her alibi was solid. Vikki had put the house on the market because she couldn't bear owning such a reminder. She'd have gladly given up all the riches in the world to have Alexis and Mike alive.

Her pulse picked up a notch. She was heating up and

unzipped her jacket. It was time to go. "I-I think I should be on my way. Thanks so much for—"

Samantha pointed at Vikki's belt. "Hey! Is that a gun you have there?"

Vikki glanced down. Her open jacket showed her holstered Glock on her belt clip. When she glanced up at their faces, John and Taylor seemed horrified.

"My grandpa carries a gun, too. Are you a police officer?" Samantha asked.

Vikki fished around for what to say.

Samantha raised a doll she was clutching in her hand. One of those American Doll types. "He gave me this for Christmas."

Vikki zipped up her jacket, stooped to the little girl's level, and smiled. "Oh, that's lovely. Yes, I'm a detective with St. Ives Police Station in New Jersey." She glanced at her parents. "I'm so sorry about that."

Taylor's face was white as snow. She waved Samantha over, her other palm placed on her chest. "Oh my God." Her voice was a whisper.

John swallowed. His Adam's apple bobbed up and down. "New Jersey, ha?"

Vikki nodded. "I should leave now. Thanks so much."

She opened the door and braced herself for the cold. Samantha was adorable—such innocence. Vikki walked toward her car, thinking of her childhood. There had never been a time she was innocent. Her childhood had been stolen from her. How lucky Samantha was to have such loving parents and grandfather.

Vikki got in her car, started the engine, and turned on the heat. She looked at the house she'd come from. Yep, someone was at the window watching. Vikki was sure Taylor and John were discussing the dangers of letting people they didn't know into the house.

She checked her phone. There was nothing from Ted. She tried his number, and it went to voice mail. Vikki wasn't worried. Work must have escalated for him. He'd call when he was free. She noticed flashing red and blue lights in her rearview mirror. Of course, they'd called the cops.

She waited, thinking of what the officer was doing. He'd probably check her plate number to see if anything was outstanding. Next, he'd come over and ask for her license, insurance, and registration. He'd run that, too. It was like shaking a tree to see if anything dislodged came down.

Vikki braced herself as the officer got out of the cruiser. A perceived false move could take everything in the wrong direction.

CHAPTER SIX

Vikki's body tensed up, a rush of heat flushing through her as her heart pounded. Taylor must have called the cops. She envisioned her on her phone saying a woman with a gun who'd said she was a detective had left her house minutes ago. New York, like New Jersey, had strict gun laws, and mentioning a weapon would put the officer on edge.

The car's vents roared in her ear. Vikki was overheated. She was about to lower it when she saw the uniform approaching in the rearview mirror, his hands by his side. She knew that stance. This was not the time for jerky movements. That was how innocent people got killed. She placed both hands on the steering wheel—took a deep breath, and let it out slowly.

She wanted to turn on the car's inner light, but again that was a sudden movement that could be misinterpreted. She waited until the uniform was by the window. It was better to follow his instructions.

He motioned with his left hand for her to lower her window. She did so.

The officer was white, maybe in his late twenties. He had

a crew cut. Ex-military, perhaps. On his winter jacket, where his breast pocket should be, was his number and the name James.

Cool air rushed in—she felt better. "Good evening, Officer. How can I help you?"

"Good evening, ma'am. License and registration, please."

Vikki lifted her hand. "I'm going to turn on the light. Is it okay?"

"Yes, ma'am."

Vikki decided to volunteer information. "I have a holstered concealed weapon on me. My license is in my purse, and my registration is in the glove compartment. I'm going to reach for the glove compartment first."

He nodded. Vikki retrieved her car registration, insurance, and license from her purse and handed them to him.

He took them with his left hand. His right brought up a flashlight. He glanced at her, then the license, comparing. "Can I see your shield?"

Vikki unclipped her detective badge from her belt. She wasn't here in an official capacity, but she wouldn't let her investigation die even before it had started. She showed it to him.

He memorized her number. "I'll be right back."

It took five minutes from when the officer walked away with her credentials to when he returned. "Do you have a concealed gun permit in New York?"

"I trained at the police academy here and worked at sixty-fourth precinct in Brooklyn before relocating to Jersey. I'm in New York only for a short time."

"Hmm. Sixty-fourth precinct, you said?"

Vikki nodded.

Officer James inhaled and exhaled. "Okay." He handed back the docs. "Everything checked out. I rarely see any cars parked here."

Maybe, but Vikki was sure Taylor had called the police. People called 911 when they had an emergency, were uncomfortable with things happening around them, or sometimes, to get the other person in trouble.

She remembered the altercation in her rookie year, a couple arguing. She'd gone to investigate. It had turned out to be more than it seemed. Within an hour of talking to that couple, her partner was dead, and her life had changed forever.

"Thank you. Happy holidays, Officer James." Vikki jerked her head toward the house. She had to know. "Did Taylor call nine-one-one?"

Officer James' cheeks turned red. "Detective Mattsen...we ensure that everything is in order. You're a long way from SIPD."

Vikki smiled. "Hmm, about an hour and thirty minutes, give or take traffic." Vikki took a deep breath and let it out in a rush. "It's the holiday season, and normally you spend it with loved ones. I grew up in that house. My family was murdered there." She saw the flicker of recognition in the officer's expression. "I hope you understand why I came."

"I'm so sorry. I heard about it. Happened before my time." He shook his head. "Nobody was apprehended. The case must be cold."

"You know whose case it is?"

Officer James shook his head. "As I said, it was before my time. But you can drop by the station. Maybe get a copy of the case file. Ask for Detective Benson. He's new. I'm sure they dumped the file on him. He's handling miscellaneous cases right now."

Vikki didn't tell him she already had the case file. It hadn't come easy either.

"You can talk to Meg. She's the department's admin. She

knows everything and is very helpful. I'll tell her you're coming."

Vikki chuckled. "We have her, too. In St. Ives, she's Jody."

A smile tugged the corner of his lip. "Or, if you give me your number, I'll ask around and get back to you."

Was he hitting on her? Since she and Ted had become an item, she'd stopped paying attention to those subtle signals given off by the opposite sex. His radio crackled.

"Come in, thirteen twenty-three."

Officer James turned to Vikki. "Duty calls. Drop by at the station. Meg will have answers. Have a good evening." He headed toward his car, speaking into his radio.

He got in. Moments later, Vikki saw the lights come on. The cruiser turned around and raced off with the siren blaring.

Vikki decided to check into a hotel before it was too late. Finding a room might be challenging with the new year approaching. The trickle-down effect from people wanting to usher in the new year in style but wanting to avoid paying Manhattan lodging fees might come as far as Long Island to find a hotel.

She headed to Garden City. There had been a cute hotel back in the day. The decor was Victorian. She hoped it was still there.

Vikki checked into The Embassy hotel, which was still luxurious but not as she remembered. Perhaps it was because she had seen authentic Victorian furniture during her sojourn in Paris and travels throughout Europe.

To keep her mind occupied, she planned to check out the Mirage, the bar Alexis had wanted them to visit. Today was her birthday, and seeing the place they'd planned on going to made a befitting tribute.

CHAPTER SEVEN

Vikki showered and shampooed, filling the bathroom with a vanilla, citrusy, flowery smell. She'd given up trying to reach Ted. She'd see him whenever. Vikki tried to recall where the Mirage was from what Alexis had said ten years ago, but only a general idea came to her—an easy job for Google Maps to solve.

The next obstacle was what to wear. Vikki emptied the content of her luggage on the king-sized framed bed. The bed, vanity mirror, and nightstand had the same intricate carved wood design painted with a gold finish. It reminded Vikki of the house in one of her cases with a murdered real estate developer.

The flat-screen showed workers at Times Square preparing for the ball drop on New Year's Eve. She pulled her eyes away and focused on her clothes. She'd put no thought into packing. All she'd wanted to do was get to Ashton and investigate, even if she had to wear the same outfit. But now she needed to visit a bar. An ordinary and shabby outfit wasn't good enough.

She picked up each item one by one. A black pantsuit, a

short black sweater dress—another pair of blue jeans, black pants, and a couple of sweaters. Worst-case scenario, she'd go to Roosevelt Field Mall and buy one or two outfits.

Thinking of the mall flooded her mind with more memories. She and Alexis had spent hours window-shopping at the stores in the mall. She remembered when they'd come across a plaque that said the mall was built on the airfield where Charles Lindbergh took off in 1927 for his solo transatlantic flight.

"It was the first nonstop flight from New York City to Paris," Alexis had said excitedly. "He named his plane the *Spirit of St. Louis.*"

Vikki's vision clouded. She wiped her eyes with the back of her hand and stared at her face in the mirror. "Alexis." She missed her a lot. She'd honor her by making up her face like Alexis, smokey eyes that made her dreamy eyes pop. She'd also try to dress like her.

She glanced at her clothes one more time and came up with the right combination, the mid-thigh black dress over blue jeans plus her suede boots.

Thirty minutes later, the GPS directed her to the parking lot of the address she'd fed into it. It was close to the outskirts of Ashton, on a street with a mixture of residential houses and businesses.

The parking lot was full, no thanks to a massive heap of snow that obliterated a section of the lot. The building had seen better days. Its better days were probably behind it. The name in front of the entrance wasn't Mirage either—it was Black Sparrow.

Pop music drifted out of the slightly open door. Vikki was thankful the music wasn't about dashing through the snow, jingle bells, or anything about Christmas. Two men and two women stood outside smoking, laughing, and chatting. She gave them a nod and went in.

The inside was like any other sports bar. It had light wood walls. About half a dozen stools, all occupied, lined the bar. Black-and-white pictures of celebrities the owner had a thing for hung on the wall, plus the obligatory swordfish. Four flat-screen TVs were strategically suspended from the ceiling so patrons could watch no matter where they sat.

Vikki had been in many bars like this, starting when she was at college. The laughter, the clinking of glasses, the anonymity of being with intimate strangers—the smells—all rushed back to her, reminding her of when she was younger. Then, it had all been fun.

After the tragedy with her family and Bruce's death—Vikki believed she was damaged goods. Anyone who tried to care for her paid the ultimate price. Instead of a relationship, she picked up men for one-night stands. But Ted had blown through that wall.

She paused for a moment. Where was he now?

There were about thirty people in the bar. Men and women sitting on the bar stools and some on high tables nursing their beverage of choice—beer, wine, spirits, or different combinations of fruit juices with alcohol. The men noticed her, and so did the women. She was pretty, her makeup was top-notch, and she was alone.

Men with partners stared at her, then looked away. The women stole glances at her. Their eyes lingered, perhaps trying to figure out what she had that made their men's eyes wander. Vikki felt good.

A man gave up his seat for her. Vikki smiled and nodded. He proceeded to an area of the bar with pool tables and a dartboard. She slipped onto the warm stool—it was comfortable. She wished she'd come here on St. Patrick's Day with Alexis. The night might have ended differently. She pushed the thought away.

Even the barman liked what he saw. He cast a flirtatious

gaze at Vikki. He was blond, square-jawed, with short, boxed stubble. He wore a black tee shirt, definitely one size smaller, showing off his cut physique and bulging biceps. He appeared younger than her, but his eyes seemed hardened.

He began to say something but stopped. "I doubt you can hear me." He leaned closer. "They like the music loud. Happy holidays. What can I get you?" He flashed her a winning smile. Before Vikki could answer, he raised a finger. "Let me guess. First, what's your name?"

Vikki thought about consuming alcohol or not. She wasn't working. She was in another jurisdiction. It was the holiday—why not. "Victoria."

His lips moved as if tasting wine, trying different variations of the shortened form. "Vic? Vikki?"

She smiled and nodded. "Vikki."

"Okay, let's guess your drink. Mai tai, a Cosmopolitan, Blue Hawaiian, Mojito, Margarita—"

Vikki raised a finger. "I'm impressed by your vast knowledge—Henny and Coke with three ice cubes will do nicely."

The man paused and drew his neck back. "A woman who knows what she wants, I like that. I'm Ringo, and I'll take care of you tonight. This is your first time here?"

It was Vikki's turn to pause. She raised an eyebrow. "Like Ringo Starr?"

"Yep, my mother has a thing for the drummer. She lives with me now. She and my sister used to say 'Star' when they talked about me and didn't want me to know." He winked.

Vikki laughed. "Ten years ago, I turned down an offer to drop by."

Ringo chuckled. "I was finishing high school then. I'm sure you weren't old enough either." He raised his head with a faraway glint in his eyes. "Ten years ago, this place was called the Mirage."

Vikki tried to control her excitement. "How did you know that?"

"My father ran it then. He died a few years ago—a heart attack. Now I'm in charge. I worked here from a young age, even in high school. I sold alcohol before I was old enough to drink."

Vikki saw the opening and took it. "This happened a long time ago. Did you hear about the girl who came here and was murdered after she left?"

"It sounds familiar. Let me think." He turned away to put her drink together.

Vikki stole glances at him. The view from behind was as good as the front. The V shape of his back tapered to a narrow waist and a tight butt covered in black leather pants.

He returned and placed a coaster and a glass of Coke and Hennessy on the bar. He invaded her personal space and said, "Why do you want to know?"

"It's a cold case I'm investigating."

"Are you with the police?"

Vikki nodded. "Detective."

He jerked back, scrutinizing her. "You have that Stana Katic thing going."

Vikki laughed. "Beckett! I catch reruns of *Castle* now and then."

"Hey, Ringo!" said a bald man sitting at the end of the bar. "I need a refill now."

"Coming up." He turned to Vikki. "I can't forget the event. It was one of those things that sunk deeper into your mind as you tried to forget. We're down one man, and the guys are thirsty tonight." He scanned the bar. "We should be done by ten. I can tell you everything you want to know after hours."

Vikki checked the time on her phone. It was almost nine.

She took a sip, then another. Her drink tasted like a splice of heaven. She drained the glass. "I can wait. Another, please."

Ringo refilled her drink, then attended to another customer. He stopped now and then to see how she was doing. By the time they closed, he'd refilled her glass four more times.

Vikki felt relaxed and free. It had been a while since she'd been at a bar on the hunt. Tonight she was hunting for information. She smiled. Ted had been her last pickup before the Trophy wife case. The more she looked at Ringo, the more appealing he became.

Vikki's old familiar urges returned. Henny and Coke had her free and loose. She glanced at Ringo and knew how the night would end.

CHAPTER EIGHT

The wall clock's short arm approached ten, and Vikki noticed the bar was almost empty. She refocused on Ringo. He methodically cleaned and shut down for the night. She'd come in for a drink or two and had almost finished a bottle of cognac. He hadn't charged her for the drinks, and Vikki wondered if he had other forms of payment in mind.

"Go on home," Ringo said to one of his workers. "I'll close for the night."

The man thanked him and left. Ringo had a contended smile. He flipped stools and placed them on the tables—like he knew the night would end in his favor. Now and then, he'd come close to her at the bar and chat, then return to shutting down.

When the last customer said their goodbyes and left, Ringo locked the front door and turned to her. "One for the road?" he said with a grin.

Vikki smiled and nodded. She wondered if she'd had a little too much but reminded herself that the only effect alcohol had on her was making her quiet and sleepy.

"So, what do you want to know?" He placed the drink before her and filled a glass of clear liquid for himself.

"You seem confident in your memory," Vikki said.

"It's been a long time, but that night changed my life." Ringo's facial expression was as serious as she'd ever seen in the few hours she'd been at his bar.

"How so?"

He raised his glass and took a sip. "The next day, after the news trickled in that one of our patrons died, I tried to guess who it was in my head, and I was thinking of someone who drank a lot that night. I came up short. Most of our regulars knew when to stop or ask for a ride home."

Despite the alcohol, Vikki's mind was alert. Perhaps her reflexes might be slowed. Was he about to confess? He seemed to have recalled a lot.

"As the day went on and more information came out, my dad said, thank God it was a home invasion and had nothing to do with us."

Vikki wanted to make sure they were on the same page. "How?"

"You know, for example, if a customer leaves here drunk and wraps his car around a tree trunk. Or, getting home and using his family as a punching bag. It comes back to bite us."

Vikki nodded. Bar owners could be held liable for injuries caused by drunk-driving accidents if they permitted visibly intoxicated persons on their premises to drive off.

Ringo took a deep breath in and exhaled loudly. He brushed his hand across his face.

Vikki's heart was pounding. He knew something. Now she wished she hadn't been cozy with Henny and Coke. Could he have done it? He'd been too young then. She lowered her right hand and bumped her elbow against her Glock. It was up to her reflexes if things went south.

"I'd forgotten about the incident until I saw her picture in the newspaper the next day."

Vikki felt like jumping to her feet, wrapping her arms around him, and urging him on. But she did not. She encouraged him with a nod.

"She sat on one of those tables, alone." Ringo gestured to a corner. "Like she was waiting for someone. I didn't serve her but remembered her because she was pretty and alone."

Vikki felt like a donkey had kicked her in the stomach. Alexis was alone because Vikki had gone to Manhattan.

"Most college kids came in groups. It was St. Patrick's Day, and I guessed maybe she was early. I went about my business. Maybe ten minutes later, when I looked in her direction, a guy was talking to her."

Adrenaline rushed through Vikki. Her pulse raced. She tried to be calm. "Can you describe him?"

Ringo shook his head. "I only saw his back. But he was dressed in jeans and a tee shirt. Maybe had on a green bowler hat."

"Did you notice anything out of the ordinary?" Vikki asked.

"She didn't seem to be enjoying the attention. She left when a bunch of college kids came in. I wondered why because I thought she'd been waiting for them. Then I had to get back to work. We scrambled to make sure we had enough drinks. They still drank the bar dry."

"Did you tell anyone of what you saw?"

Ringo pursed his lips, resting his elbows on the bar. "I told my dad. He said if the police came, I should tell them what I saw. But if they didn't ask, I shouldn't volunteer half-baked information. God help us if the person committed the murders after a few drinks from here."

Vikki knew the answer but asked anyway. "Did the police interview you?"

He shook his head. "No. They never came to the bar. After a few weeks, everything died down, and people moved on. It's been on my conscience since, and here you are, talking about it."

A few seconds passed, and none of them spoke. A car honked three times.

Ringo leaned off the bar. "That's my ride." He opened his palms. "Keys, please."

Vikki batted her eyelids. "What?"

"I'm not letting you drive after putting a dent in my bottle of Hennessy. You have three options. One, I'll drive you to where you're staying. John will follow us in your car and pick me up. In case you're wondering, John is my husband. He's the one honking outside. Two, we call an Uber. Three, we drop you off at your hotel, and you pick up your car tomorrow morning."

Vikki waved a hand in dismissal. "I'm fine. I can handle my alcohol." She was disappointed. He played for the other team, but it was all good. Those erotic thoughts were now far from her mind. "You guys must have had video cameras."

Ringo laughed. "We still do. But ten years ago, we had VHS tapes. My dad was old school. He believed in tangible things."

Vikki felt a surge of hope. The tapes may be stored somewhere.

"Our videos were dubbed over every twenty-four hours. Moreover, those videotapes must be in a landfill somewhere."

Vikki's hopes deflated. The car honked again.

"Thank you, though," Vikki said. "At least I have some questions for the police." She slipped off her stool and felt lightheaded. She took a step. It felt like she had a live rehearsal of The Beatles playing inside her head.

Vikki's mind was sharp, but maybe she'd overdone it. She inhaled and exhaled and tried to appear in control. She felt she could drive, but what if something went wrong and she ended up in a ditch? The attention wouldn't do her any favors.

She brought out her cell phone and tapped the screen. "I'll hail an Uber. Will my car be safe here?"

"As long as it's not a Bentayga." Ringo opened his palm. "Keys, please."

CHAPTER NINE

Ringo's husband was a big muscular white guy, soft-spoken and concerned about Vikki's welfare. He admonished Ringo for letting her drink as much as she had. They dropped Vikki off at The Embassy. They didn't drive off until she waved and entered the hotel lobby.

The heat from an artificial fire in the fireplace next to a tall Christmas tree engulfed her. It filled the lounge with warmth and the sounds of crackling wood.

Vikki retrieved her phone from her purse for the time; almost eleven. She had a few missed calls and text messages too. She'd check them out in her room.

The receptionist, a brunette in her later thirties, looked up from a paperback, smiled, and continued reading. Vikki walked over to the closet-sized room next to the receptionist that served as a store. She took a bottle of water from the fridge and contemplated getting a bar of Almond Joy. She decided against it. Maybe in the morning. Instead, she picked up three sachets of painkillers.

"Charge it to my room, please," Vikki said to the receptionist as she resurfaced from her book again.

"Room number, please?"

Vikki told her. The woman, it seemed, wanted to say more, but Vikki was tired and headed for the elevator. She pushed the "up" button and heard the familiar rumble of pulleys as the elevator came to life.

A sudden movement in her periphery caught her attention. Someone stood and walked toward her.

Vikki put the bottle of water in the left pocket of her jacket and unzipped it. She didn't want to be hindered if she had to go for her gun. The figure approached from her right. Her mouth dropped open when he got closer.

"T-Ted! What are you doing here?" His white long-sleeved tee shirt underneath sky-blue scrubs suggested he came straight from work. His puffy jacket was draped over his arm.

He gave her a shy smile. "I thought I heard your voice. I've been trying to reach you."

Shame washed over Vikki. What if she'd walked in here with Ringo? Or she hadn't come back at all? Before she put her foot in her mouth, the elevator dinged, and the door slid open.

Vikki cocked her head toward the elevator. "Let's go up."

She stepped in, and Ted followed. She'd never been so uncomfortable. It reminded her of her first dates in high school. Not sure of what to say in case she said the wrong thing.

"You were finally able to escape?" she said.

Ted chuckled. "Escape is the right word. Today was one of those days the job got to me."

"Oh no, what was the case? I thought it was always like checking under the hood of a different car. How did you describe it again?"

Ted was resting his back on the wall of the elevator. His feet crossed at the ankle, his hands grasping onto his jacket in front of him. He stared at his shoes and sighed. "I worked on a family that won't see the new year. Two little kids with their parents. A drunk, driving against a one-way road, plowed into them at full speed." He shook his head. "The only consolation was the end came fast for them."

Vikki's heart seemed to drop to the pit of her stomach. She was about to go to him and remembered. She'd been drinking, too. Only she'd had the fortitude not to drive. "I'm so sorry." Instinctively, she covered her mouth with her hand. She didn't want him to smell the alcohol on her breath.

The elevator stopped, and the door slid open.

"This way." Vikki got out, made a left, and headed down a corridor to her door. She removed the key card from her pocket and let them in.

"Goodness." She'd forgotten she'd left the room in a mess. Her clothes were strewn all over the bed. She threw them back into the suitcase. "Sorry about that."

Ted waved a hand and sat on the bed. "So, what have you been up to?"

Vikki started from when she'd arrived and went to her old house. She talked about the neighbor watching her through the window from the house across the street. She'd gone there and learned that the new owner lived abroad. The house was empty.

"Does that mean anything?"

"Nothing I can think of," Vikki said, shaking her head. "Anyway, they called the cops on me after I left."

Ted raised an eyebrow. "Friendly neighbors. You told him you are a New Jersey detective?"

Vikki shrugged. "He ran my plate and license, and I showed my badge. He said to drop by the station if I needed more information."

Ted nodded.

Now the tricky part. She had to come clean. What could have happened if Ringo wasn't gay? She swallowed. "Do you want a drink?" Vikki walked over to the mini fridge and opened it. There was a small Poland Spring bottle. She took it, handed it to Ted, and sat beside him on the bed.

He broke the seal and raised the bottle to his lips. He didn't let it down until it was empty. "I didn't know I was thirsty." He crushed the bottle in his palm. "What else did you learn?"

"I decided to check out the sports bar Alexis had invited me to that day ten years ago. In honor of her birthday."

"That's nice," Ted said.

"I-I met the bartender." Vikki gestured with her thumb in the general direction she felt the bar was located. This was her time to come clean. She skipped it. "Funny, he remembered the incident like it was yesterday."

"Was he sure? Or was he trying to separate you from your underwear?"

Vikki's cheeks burned. It was the opposite. She wanted to say, at a point, he could have. Instead, she said, "He remembered her because he thought she was waiting for her friends but left after a group of college kids walked in. But before then, he'd seen a guy talking to her. She blew him off and left. The next day, he heard she was dead."

Ted raised his head. "The software that can age people has improved over the years. Do you have a description?"

"No, he only saw his back. They threw away the video tapes when they switched to cloud storage."

Ted exhaled like a balloon letting out air. "I hate when that happens."

"But it raised a question for me," Vikki said. "We had a video camera in the home back then, focused on the front door. It wasn't mentioned in the case file." She turned to Ted. "Do you remember coming across it when you read the file?"

Ted thought for a moment. "I can't say for sure. Maybe I missed it. I'll reread it."

Vikki nodded. "That's what I plan to do tonight. Then tomorrow, I'll go talk to the detective at the police station."

Ted massaged her shoulders with both hands.

Vikki shut her eyes. She felt hot all over. A fluttery sensation began in her chest and spread to her stomach. She threw her head back and sighed. "That feels so good." She let him go on, then sprang to her feet. "Let's not get carried away." Sex with Ted would leave her exhausted.

She walked to her suitcase, removed the case file from a zippered partition, and glanced at him. "I'm going to change and start reading." She saw the desire in his eyes and turned away. Minutes ago, she'd been ready to sleep with someone else. Now she blamed exhaustion.

Ted raised his hand, clutched his head with both palms, and fell back on the bed.

Vikki dropped the file on the table, fished out her nightgown, and headed for the bathroom.

Ted sighed. "I'll catch some sleep. Wake me up when you're done reading."

CHAPTER TEN

Vikki retrieved the bottle of water she'd stowed in her jacket pocket and took a long drink. Beside her, Ted snored. She watched him, wondering if he and Alexis would've gotten along. Probably.

Vikki didn't know why she felt so destructive tonight. Her actions were similar to pulling the pin from a grenade, tossing it into one's closet, and waiting to see what happened next. She still had Ted in her life because he was stubborn and refused to leave because he felt something more for her. But one could only take so much. Was she taking him for granted? Vikki shook her head and refocused on the case folder.

She took her time reading the report and looking for any mention of a video camera in their home. The more she read, the surer she was they'd had a camera. By the time she came to the end of the case file, an hour was gone, and she was sleepy. And there was no mention of any cameras or video tapes recovered from the scene.

The hotel room was quiet, the silence punctuated by the humming of the fridge. Vikki was drifting off and contemplated calling it a night when a voice said, "So, why weren't you a suspect in the murders?"

Her head jerked up, eyes zeroed in on Ted's. "I thought you were asleep."

"Snoozing," Ted said. "You should have been the number one suspect. You had a lot to gain."

Vikki stared at Ted. She was wide awake like fog vanishing from a windshield. "What...what do you mean?"

"Walk me through what happened that night. So, Alexis invited you to hang out with her, but you left her and went to the city. Take it from there."

Time stood still—a painful lump formed in Vikki's throat. Ted should have punched her in the chest. It would probably hurt less than his words.

She swallowed. "Some of my modeling friends had traveled from Paris with me. I told them I'd return later that night to check on them and show them around. Alexis mentioned going to the sports bar, and I told her about my friends in the city. I was back in the country for good. We could go some other time. I went to Manhattan, and Alexis went to the bar alone."

Ted sat up and leaned back on his elbow, watching Vikki.

"I took a yellow cab from the city. I saw the lights as we got closer to the house. A police cruiser blocked the street. I paid the cab driver off and walked the rest of the way. That was when I realized the activity was in our driveway. I thought it was a fallout from the fundraiser. Someone had too much to drink and got in a fight. The police stopped me. And when I said it was my home, they pulled me aside and called Levin."

Ted raised an eyebrow. "St. Ives, Captain Levin?"

Vikki nodded. "He told me what happened and needed to ask me some questions. A uniform took me to the station, and they put me in an interview room." She drank from her water bottle. "My decision to go to the city gave me the strongest alibi. I couldn't be in two places at the same time. People in Manhattan remembered us. Young, beautiful, noisy women enjoying a girls' night out. We took pictures everywhere with time and date stamps." Her limps trembled.

"If you hadn't hung out with your friends, you'd have gone out with Alexis," Ted said.

"And she'd be alive," Vikki said in a shaky voice.

"Or, you'd have met the same fate as they did," Ted said, his voice quiet. "Did you find anything about the video camera in the file?"

"No. I'm sure the investigators must have come across it. But I don't know why it wasn't mentioned."

Ted reached for the folder and leafed through it. "What if it wasn't there anymore? Maybe Mike Devoe had removed the camera while you were in Paris?"

Vikki shook her head. "Removed? No way. Nobody does that. Possibly upgraded it."

Nodding, Ted sighed. "I agree with you. Why don't you get some sleep? I'll read through it. If we come to the same conclusion, the detective who handled the case can throw more light on it tomorrow."

Vikki felt better. Ted tucked her in, kissed her on the cheek, and took the file to the table. He turned off the lamps on the nightstand and read the folder with the table lamp. She could barely keep her eyes open. Soon, she was fast asleep.

When Vikki woke in the morning, she was well-rested and overcome by the desire for morning sex. Eyes still closed, she ran her hand along the other side of the bed. It was empty, and the sheets were cold. Was he still reading the case? Her eyes popped open, and her gaze darted to the reading desk. He was not there. She checked the room. It was empty.

"Ted?"

No answer. The door to the bathroom was open. Vikki needed to pee and headed for the bathroom. Nobody was there either. Ted was gone.

CHAPTER ELEVEN

She'd woken up to discover that Ted had returned to St. Ives. He'd left a lengthy note. Vikki's heart raced as she read it.

Got a call from dispatch—another accident on the highway with fatalities. If only people swapped their alcohol of choice for the ambrosia Greek gods had in mind, more people would make it to the new year. Camera or feed not mentioned in the case file. Bring it up with the detective at the station. I'll call once I get a chance. Love, Ted.

Vikki's lungs burned from holding her breath. He'd left because of work. She brushed her teeth, showered, and dressed in her black pantsuit and a blue shirt. She looked more like a banker than a detective. The case file went into a tote she'd brought along. She left her room, put the Do Not Disturb sign on, and headed for the elevator.

In the lobby, the smell of coffee guided her to the hotel's complimentary breakfast. She had coffee, eggs, sausages, and pancakes. She focused on her food, not paying attention to other guests as they spoke and dug into their food.

She finished breakfast. It was time to head to the police station. The automatic doors in the lobby opened for her, and she stepped outside. Cold air wrapped around her like a wet blanket. She must get to her car before her ears froze. Vikki scanned the parking lot. "Damn." Her car hadn't made it home with her.

She placed a call to Ringo with her fingers crossed. People who worked nights slept in. She hoped Ringo was the outlier.

Ringo answered on the third ring. "I got out of the gym right now. I'm sweaty and need to shower first."

Vikki explained she needed to be somewhere by nine. She could come to him to get her key.

"Meet me at the bar in ten minutes," Ringo said.

Vikki hailed an Uber with her phone, which took its sweet time to get to her. Her car was where she'd left it when she reached the bar, but no Ringo. She tried the door to the bar. It was locked.

Vikki had already dismissed the Uber driver. She called Ringo. "Where are you?"

"I'm about to get in the shower."

Vikki shut her eyes and blocked everything out. She filled her lungs with cold air and let it out slowly. She reconnected with Ringo.

"Did you find it? I left the key fob on top of the back passenger tire."

She did. Her lips trembled. Her fingers hurt—a white cloud formed each time she exhaled.

Vikki fed the address of the Ashton Police Station into her phone's GPS. She was delighted she recognized some locations. They were slightly different but hadn't changed much.

"Your destination is ten minutes away," said the female mechanical GPS voice.

Vikki took a deep breath and let it out in a rush. Her ETA was nine a.m. That was good timing, considering how her morning had taken off. The GPS was the only thing consistent this morning so far.

It was one of the coldest drives in her life. Now, she was at her destination.

Vikki turned into the parking lot of the police station. She found a spot, checked herself in the rearview mirror one last time, and exited the car.

She marched up the stairs and entered the reception area. She couldn't remember her visit ten years ago, but there was this déjà vu feeling. Someone once said that no matter where you are in the world, police stations give off the same vibe. She agreed.

The customary shabby Christmas tree stood in a corner. A bench resembling a church pew faced a glass window in the wall. To the left of the glass window was a door with a keypad. Behind the glass was a man in uniform. He was tired, with bags under his eyes.

"Good morning. How can I help you?"

Vikki smiled. "Hi, I'm here to see Meg." She cursed herself for not getting a last name. "My name is Victoria Mattsen."

The officer's eyes lit up. "Yes. Meg is not here today. But Officer James told me you'd be dropping by. Detective Benson is who you'll be meeting. If you can take a seat." He pointed at the bench behind Vikki. "I'll be with you shortly."

Vikki nodded her thanks and sat. She was expected. That was nice of the patrol officer from last night to have set it up.

Five minutes later, the door with a combination lock opened. A man dressed in a black suit came through. He seemed over six feet tall, in his sixties, with male-pattern baldness and graying at the temples.

"Detective Mattsen?" The man's voice was deep and rumbling.

"Yes." Vikki got up from her seat.

The man extended his hand. "I'm Captain Miller Lloyd. Captain Levin speaks very highly of you."

Vikki shook his hand and tried to hide her confusion. She'd been expecting a detective. And she had also specifically asked Chief Levin not to intervene on her behalf. Did that mean Levin knew she was in New York? Right now, she was AWOL.

"Neil and I go back a long way." He punched some numbers into the door's keypad and then opened it. "Please, this way."

Captain Lloyd led the way to an elevator. They rode up one floor. They passed an open door. The number of tables with monitors on them and a few men and women in civilian garb with holsters was a dead giveaway—the detective squad room.

Captain Lloyd ushered her into his office. It was conservatively furnished—an executive desk with a computer monitor and phone on it— was almost placed against the wall facing the door, with three leather chairs on the opposite side. On a bookshelf against the wall were several framed photos. A picture of him, and a woman, probably his wife. And another of a little girl of about seven.

Instead of a couch and coffee table, he had a miniature version of a conference room in his office. A table, large enough to accommodate six people, stood at the center with a speakerphone positioned on it.

"Please sit." He pointed at one of the leather chairs opposite his. "Can I get you something—coffee, tea, water?"

"No, thank you."

He sat.

Vikki believed she was better off talking to the man handling the case. The captain might know only a little about the murders.

"Sir, I know you're busy, and considering today is New Year's Eve, I don't want to take up your time. I was told a Detective Benson—"

Captain Lloyd waved a dismissive hand. "Don't worry—they'll let us know once he arrives." He smiled. "I'm not supposed to say this, but Neil did talk to me about you. When I heard you were in the building, I said why not meet you. He said he convinced you to join the police force first, then seek revenge later."

That story embarrassed Vikki whenever it was told. It made her come across as a brat, not in touch with reality.

The captain nodded. "I'm so sorry for your loss. We were all there that day."

Vikki, who'd been searching for an excuse to get away from the office, was now interested in staying. "You were there?"

Captain Lloyd pursed his lips and gave a subtle nod. "Every officer who wasn't tied down was there. It was a shame." He made a steeple with his hands. "I have a question for you. It's been so many years. Why now?"

Vikki was quiet. All that hidden emotion surged to the surface. She must not cry. She swallowed and blinked rapidly. "Mike Devoe was a father to me. Alexis, a sister. Yesterday was her birthday. She'd have been thirty-two." Her voice was firm, which surprised her. It gave her the courage to say more. "She saved my life, saved me from the foster system. I couldn't have survived it. I promised her justice once I had the training." She laughed. "It's been a decade already. We become complacent and tend to be comfortable where we are. I think I've learned enough to examine what happened critically."

Captain Lloyd cleared his throat. "I understand what you mean."

Vikki contemplated mentioning that the case file had taken a long time to get to her. The person who'd dropped the ball might be reprimanded. Vikki killed the thought fast. She needed corporation from the Ashton police, not witch-hunting.

The phone on the table rang.

Captain Lloyd raised a finger. "One second." He picked up the receiver. "Lloyd." He listened and nodded a few times. "Thank you." He put the receiver down. "Benson is on his way up."

Moments later, there was a knock on the door.

Vikki turned toward the door to see a man walk in.

Captain Lloyd got up. "Detective Mattsen, this is Detective Ron Benson. He'll be in a better position to help you." The captain opened a drawer on his table. He brought out a business card and passed it to Vikki. "If you need anything, please do not hesitate to ask."

CHAPTER TWELVE

Ron Benson led the way out of Captain Lloyd's office. He was probably in his late thirties, above average height, dark-skinned with an athletic build. Dressed in a navy-blue suit, white shirt, and red tie, he'd pass for a politician running for office.

Detective Benson smiled. "You must be a morning person." He had a Southern accent.

"Kind of. It depends on what the plan for the day is and how early I went to bed the night before."

"Sounds like me."

Detective Benson led the way. They seemed to be going to the squad room she'd passed earlier with the captain.

Vikki glanced at him. "Thanks so much for coming out this early."

"I was going to be here anyway."

His face and head were clean-shaven. A scar ran from his left temple to the top of his ear. She wondered what had happened. He caught her staring.

"My scar? A hair's breadth to the right, and I'd have been maggot chow."

Vikki bit her tongue before she asked the follow-up question everyone must have asked him. How did it happen?

Detective Benson volunteered. "I used to be in the military, military police stationed in Afghanistan. Our convoy was ambushed on a routine patrol. Hot lead flew everywhere. I was lucky. I only got a permanent haircut. Some didn't make it."

"I'm sorry to hear that," Vikki said. She was curious, too. "How does it work? I mean, going from military police to detective?"

Detective Ron chuckled. "No. I went to the police academy. I did all the training. Physical, firearms, scenario-based training, the written exams—the whole nine yards. Maybe they only skipped the background check. The process took almost a year." He entered the squad room.

Vikki followed.

Three men and a woman sat at their desks typing away on their keyboards. None glanced up. Detective Benson walked over to a desk. He moved folders on a chair and placed them on the table.

He brushed off the chair with his palm. "Please."

"Thank you." Vikki sat. "What should I call you?"

"Ron is fine. What about you?"

"Vikki. Short for Victoria."

Ron sat and frowned. He pointed at Vikki. "Are you the Victoria mentioned in the case file?"

Vikki nodded. "That's me. That's why I'm here."

"I'm so sorry. It was...it was terrible what happened. Can I get you something to drink? Tea. Coffee."

"Maybe later," Vikki said. She was tired of saying no all the time. "I have a few questions. I've reviewed the case file several times and had another set of eyes go through it. We had a video camera in the house. There was no mention of it in the report. I know one was outside and caught whoever came to the door. There's no way it couldn't have captured who committed the crime."

Detective Edwards cocked his head. He reached for a pile of files on his table and pulled one out. "I went through this several times myself. I don't recall a camera." He opened the folder and turned a few pages. "Are you sure?"

Vikki's eyes narrowed.

Ron dipped his chin. "Of course you are. No offense intended."

"None taken."

"But why are you interested in the investigation now? It's been what, nine to ten years since."

"Captain Lloyd asked me the same thing," Vikki said. She took a deep breath and blew it out through her mouth. She told him exactly what she'd said to the captain. Alexis' birthday was her trigger, and she'd earned the skills to do something about it.

Ron kept on nodding.

Vikki glanced down at her hands. Despite her years of experience, a cold case was always formidable. But after reading the case file, she was hopeful. Her eyes met Ron's. "What do you think?"

"About the case?"

Vikki raised an eyebrow. *Of course. What else?* She wanted to say. Instead, she said, "Yes."

"Well, for starters, I'm the new kid on the block."

"Right, and I'm Beyoncé."

"What?" Ron laughed. "What do I think?" He took a deep breath and exhaled.

Vikki leaned forward. "Could part of the file be missing? Or, for some reason, it was not documented?"

Detective Benson raised both hands. "I can't say. I was hired because of my military background—my experiences with firearms and having seen active combat. Both drug and gang problems are becoming major issues in the suburbs. The plan is for the department to be ready for any showdown."

Vikki could relate to that. They'd taken down a major drug distributor in St. Ives operating under their noses.

"I've been sitting on my hands since I was hired, tagging along on other cases until about two weeks ago." He glanced around and lowered his voice. "In retrospect, I think from talking to you now, that was when I was given the case. And I think that was when you requested the file."

Vikki was interested. "Two or three weeks ago, I heard from someone in the department acknowledging receiving my request."

"I got the case, a cold case. I was excited."

Vikki didn't know why he was excited, but she didn't ask. It was an open secret that the longer it took to solve a crime, the more likely it never would be.

"The guy who worked on it is retired and moved to the Sunshine State. I was told to familiarize myself with it. I read through it, and when I was done, I was told about the confession."

Vikki blinked. She didn't think she'd heard right. "Say it again."

"The confession to the murder."

Vikki's heartbeat pounded like a subway train rumbling in the tunnel under 42nd Street. "Someone confessed to the murder?"

Detective Ron Benson nodded slowly. "Yeah, some guy already doing life at Nassau County Correctional Facility confessed to the murders. It went from cold to closed."

Vikki couldn't believe what she'd heard. Someone had confessed? Why hadn't Captain Lloyd told her? He wanted it to be a surprise? Vikki realized that Detective Benson was still talking and refocused on him.

"The prisoner's name is Edward Poole."

"What was his crime?" Vikki asked. Her voice was barely audible.

"A liquor store was held up in Hempstead by two men. A new store clerk went after them."

Vikki shook her head. That was a no-no. Whatever they stole could be replaced. She knew where the story was headed.

"Mr. Poole pumped three shots into the store clerk. One of the bullets tore off his aorta. He didn't have a chance. That happened a few days after the Devoe case."

Vikki massaged her temples. A monster headache was brewing. Why hadn't she been notified right away?

"This happened two days ago. I'm scheduled to see Mr. Poole today by twelve-thirty p.m. Appointments are made in advance. I don't know if they'll let you in. But you're welcome to come with me and try your luck."

Vikki couldn't believe it. A confession? This she must hear herself. She was aware that prisons loved to know who was visiting in advance. She also knew someone with clout talking to the warden might get her in. Captain Lloyd came to mind. She reached into her coat pocket for his business card.

Detective Benson picked up the receiver of his phone. "I could try to add you."

Vikki held up the business card. "Wait. Captain Lloyd said to call him if I needed anything."

Ron shrugged. "Why not. If you can reach him, I'm sure he'll try."

Vikki punched in his number on her cell phone. Each time she heard the ringing tone, her headache got worse. The captain answered on the third ring.

"Detective Mattsen?"

Vikki's pulse raced. "Yes."

Captain Lloyd gave a cheerful laugh. "It took me a

moment to place the name on the screen. How can I help you?"

Vikki told him. She refrained from asking why he hadn't told her about the confession.

"Not a problem. I'll call the warden. You'll only hear from me if there's one."

Vikki thanked him and hung up. She relayed what he'd said to Ron.

"Nice. Before we go, do you have any questions about Poole?"

"Do you know what he got in return? Poole wasn't going anywhere."

Detective Benson placed his elbows on the desk and interlocked his fingers. "I don't know. Maybe he was seeking forgiveness or redemption. Maybe for improved living conditions, to gain notoriety amongst other prisoners, or he felt remorseful."

Vikki nodded. Her request for the case file had set things in motion. "I guess we'll hear from the horse's mouth."

"From my military experience, families like to know what happened to their father, son, or daughter to get closure. Maybe that's what the culprit is trying to do. To provide closure. But as you said, we'll hear from him."

CHAPTER THIRTEEN

Snow was coming down when they got to the car park. Detective Benson drove a Red Jeep Cherokee. He'd remote-started it and turned on the heat before they got in. Vikki was thankful for that.

"It's a twenty-minute drive, give or take, to East Meadow," Detective Benson said. "It might take a little longer with the weather."

As they drove, the snow transitioned from a heavy down-fall to intermittent flurries before finally ceasing. Crazy thoughts bounced around Vikki's head like the ball in a pinball machine. Its direction altered by whatever it struck as it rolled down. Had Captain Levin asked Lloyd for a favor—to the case?

Detective Benson took his eyes off the road for a second. "Do you have family in New York?"

"Not that I know of."

Detective Benson chuckled. "You, are funny."

Vikki knew she had distant relatives she'd never met on her mother's side. Before the Devoes had taken her in, she'd known only her biological parents, then her stepfather. She didn't want to talk about her family. Detective Benson must have sensed she wasn't in a sharing mood and backed away.

What would she do when she saw the killer of her family face to face? A chill traveled down Vikki's spine. The man had denied her the joy of growing older with people who loved her. That cut short her second chance at a family. She might shoot the bastard. It was a good thing they were not allowed to bring in firearms.

As Vikki and Ron approached, the large concrete building loomed before them. They walked up to the front entrance and were greeted by a guard who asked for their identification. After verifying their information, the guard directed them to the visitors' area.

Another guard said, "Do you have any weapons on you?"

Ron nodded. "We're both detectives. We have our firearms."

"We'll have to check them in," the guard said. "Any knives?"

They both shook their heads.

They didn't take their word for it. Like with TSA at the airports, Vikki and Ron passed through a metal detector before being allowed to enter the visitors' room.

They were not the only people in the waiting area. There were men and women, old and young. Little children, too. All were there to wish their family members a happy New Year.

They waited for their turn. The little ones, bored out of their minds, skipped around with their parent, guardian, or older sibling, trying to call them to order. After about an hour, it was their turn.

The room they were in was empty but for a table and three chairs—reserved for meetings between inmates and their lawyers. Where discussions were private. Vikki and Detective Benson sat on one side of the table.

A few minutes later, the door on the opposite side to the

one they'd walked in from opened, and a guard led a prisoner in. He wore an orange jumpsuit with his hands cuffed in front of him and his feet shackled. He shuffled toward the table.

Edward Poole was in his early thirties, chiseled with thick black hair and crazy eyes. He glanced at Detective Benson, then his eyes traveled to Vikki, and his gaze settled on her.

Vikki's fists were clenched tight. She wanted to scream and lash out at the man who'd ended the lives of those dear to her—but she also needed to know why he'd done what he had. The guard directed him to the chair opposite them.

Detective Benson wasted no time in getting down to business. "Mr. Poole, I'm Detective Ron Benson with Ashton PD. This is my colleague, Detective Victoria Mattsen. She's with SIPD. Thanks very much for— "

"What's SIPD?" Mr. Poole asked.

Vikki cleared her throat. "St. Ives Police Department, New Jersey."

The prisoner frowned. "New Jersey? I never committed a crime in New Jersey." His voice was melodious, his words drawn out.

"Sticking to that subject, can you work us through what happened that day ten years ago, March seventeenth?"

Mr. Poole smiled. "Like I told my lawyer, I saw the girl at the bar. It was love at first sight. I talked to her, and she brushed me off like I was a mosquito, a bug." He placed both palms on his chest with a rattle of chains. "She broke my heart."

Vikki was boiling inside as she watched him calmly recount the story like he was teaching Sunday school.

"It was St. Patrick's Day—I drank a lot. I'd forgotten about her. I went to pee, and as I came back—boom. I saw her leaving. I followed her. I'd bought a six-pack earlier. I grabbed one from the backseat and drank as I drove. She drives up a driveway and into the garage. I couldn't follow, so

I parked on the street. People were still up in the house. I must have dozed off because most of the lights in the house were out."

Detective Benson interrupted him. "What time was this?"

Poole Shrugged. "I don't know. It was late. Nine, ten."

"What did you do then?" Vikki asked with iciness in her voice.

"I drank some more. I saw the girl by the window, and I felt horny." He glared at Vikki.

A painful lump formed in Vikki's throat. Her stomach tightened. She didn't want to hear this, but she had to. "Continue."

"I opened the glove compartment and grabbed my gun."

"What for?" Detective Benson asked.

Poole shook his head. "I don't know. My dick was doing the thinking." He swallowed. "I rang the bell and waited. I heard footsteps coming. The door opened. She was smiling—like she was expecting me. Her smile faded. It wasn't for me. She tried to close the door. I shoved the gun in her face, pushed her back, and shut the door."

Vikki's heart was pounding. Her hands trembled. She placed them on her knees and squeezed. Did she have to listen to this?

Poole continued. "She begged me not to hurt her. Then a man appeared on the stairs, yelling at me. I shot him, and she screamed even louder. I told her to shut up. I was scared somebody else might hear. But she refused to listen. I wrestled her to the floor—covered her mouth with my hand. She struggled for some time, then stopped. By then, it was too late."

Vikki's vision was clouded with unshed tears. Alexis' and her father's deaths were so tragic. She hoped they hadn't suffered much. Knowing was supposed to give her closure, but Vikki wasn't satisfied. It felt like a Pyrrhic victory, and his story seemed...too structured.

Detective Benson leaned closer to Vikki. "Do...do you have any more questions for him?" His voice was almost a whisper.

Vikki stared at Poole, then said, "When you walked into the foyer, did the statue startle you?"

Poole's eyes narrowed. "W-what?"

"Maybe it had been removed. The statue in the foyer."

Poole went utterly still. "Which statue?"

"It was St. Patrick's Day."

Poole thought for a moment. He licked his lips, then smacked his forehead with the heel of his palm. "The leprechaun mannequin. Yup, it was there."

"Are you sure?" Vikki asked.

"Yes. It had on a green suit."

Vikki stared at him, nostrils flaring. She sprang to her feet. Her chair made a scraping noise on the tiled floor. "That will be all." She headed for the door.

Poole got up. "Hey! Where are you going?"

The guard was beside him in a heartbeat.

"We're not done," Poole said. "It's supposed to—"

"I think we are," Detective Benson said. He got up and headed for the door.

Vikki turned at the door ad locked eyes with the prisoner.

Mr. Poole let out a sigh. "I-I thought this was, how do you say it...a conjugal visit."

CHAPTER FOURTEEN

Vikki resisted the urge to turn. She knew Ron Benson was coming after her.

"Detective. Hold up."

Vikki slowed, then stopped. Her chest rose and fell as if she'd just finished a fifty-meter dash.

"What happened in there?"

Vikki didn't want to make it weird. "I'm sorry—my fault. I shouldn't have gotten upset."

Detective Benson threw up his hands. "I still don't understand what happened. You sat there listening, asking the right questions, then boom. You got up and left."

Vikki looked around. "Not here."

They cleared security, retrieved their weapons and jacket, and headed for the parking lot. This time the car was cold. Detective Benson hadn't had enough time to warm it up.

He started the car and set the heater to high. "So, what happened back there?"

Vikki had been thinking about it. Something was not adding up. At first, they'd held on to the case file. After some delays, they released it. She'd showed up, and out of the blue, there had been a confession. Was there a cover-up? Could Detective Benson be a part of it? He was new to the department. Her gut feeling said he wasn't.

"You're not going to tell me?"

Vikki gave a half-hearted shrug. "He wasn't there. He wasn't in the house. I think someone is trying to make me accept the wrong conclusion."

Detective Benson's head jerked to face her. He was quiet for half a minute. "That's a tough allegation." He lowered the heather.

Vikki warmed up fast, like the car. Their only companion was the hum of the Cherokee engine and the barely audible jingle from the radio.

Detective Benson said, "You have to think this through." His voice was quiet, serious sounding. "You can't say this out loud without expecting some blowback. How did you get to that conclusion?"

"There was a life-size statue of the goddess, Venus de Milo, in the foyer. It's six feet eight inches tall. It's tough to miss, especially with her torso exposed and her arms missing."

Detective Edwards tapped a finger on his lips. "Poole was on a mission and already had a gun. His sights were on a living female. It's possible he didn't see the statue. You know, tunnel vision—adrenaline and all that."

Vikki thought for a moment. That could be debated. There was always another side to every coin. If they had the security footage, there wouldn't be any ambiguity.

"What are you going to do?"

Vikki felt like a chicken in a pressure cooker—trapped. Heat cascaded through her body. She zipped down her jacket. "I don't know."

"Remember, the police is a hierarchical system like the

military. Your superiors have the power to make or break your career."

Vikki wanted to protest that she wasn't a part of the Ashton police department, but Edwards beat her to it.

"The case was cold for a decade until you asked for the files. Then there was a confession, the murders solved, and the case closed." He cocked his head. "It's suspicious, but it could mean nothing. Maybe someone did a sloppy job, or there was a cover." He exhaled. "I'm a soldier, trained to obey the last command." A burst of nervous laughter escaped his lips. "All I'm trying to say is tread lightly."

Vikki nodded. "Why don't we go back to the station so I can get my car."

"Sure." He backed out of the parking lot and joined the traffic.

The drive back was quiet. Vikki was glad the Christmas jingles were done with. Then she remembered it was New Year's Eve, too. She didn't know what to do. Talk to Lloyd again or the detective in Florida who'd handled the case. Maybe there were things he didn't want to write down but was willing to discuss.

Detective Benson drove into the police department's parking lot. He found a spot. "What's the next plan?"

Vikki shook her head. "I don't know. Nothing I do will bring my loved ones back. Someone cut their lives short. All I want is accountability. Injustice anywhere is a threat to justice everywhere."

"Martin Luther King Jr., right?"

Vikki nodded.

"I'm sorry. I shouldn't see this as your problem. Disregard the hierarchy thing I said. The community does not heal until those unaffected are as outraged as those who are."

Vikki smile. "Well said."

Detective Benson checked the time on his watch. "Time

flies when you're having fun. It's already five. Now that we're done reciting quotes, do you have any plans for the night?"

Vikki wanted to get back to her room and take a shower. Since meeting Poole, she'd felt filthy. She was about to say she wasn't sure when it hit her. "Are you asking me out?"

Detective Benson smiled sheepishly. "We can usher in the new year together."

Vikki thought about Ted. She should be with him. Maybe Poole was indeed the murderer—case closed. Vikki cocked her head. "Thanks, but my guy already asked me. I think I'll head back to Jersey and come back in the new year to follow up on the case."

Edward's raised his hand in surrender. "Okay." He opened his dash and gave Vikki his business card. "Call or text me if you have any questions. Remember, the case is closed."

Vikki put the card in her pocket with Captain Lloyd's. She thanked him again and got out. She headed toward her car and watched Edward's vehicle drive away. Once she started her car, she cranked up the heat.

Vikki drove to her hotel. Maybe Ted was right after all. She should return to St. Ives and spend New Year's Eve with him. Watch the ball drop at Times Square from the comfort of their living room. In the new year, they could take time off as initially planned.

Back in the hotel, she crossed the lobby heading to the elevator when the receptionist called out.

"Ms. Mattsen."

Vikki stopped and glanced her way. She flashed her a smile. "Yes."

The receptionist pointed. "A gentleman is waiting for you at the lounge."

"Me?"

The lady nodded.

Vikki saw only one person, and he was facing away from

her. He turned around to the sound of her footsteps. She stopped, not believing her eyes. She knew he was her visitor. The man had given her stress for the past seven years, and there he was, smiling at her.

"Hello, Vikki.

"Detective McClane, this is a surprise."

CHAPTER FIFTEEN

Vikki was lost for words. "What...what are you doing here? What do you want?"

Detective McClane brushed off invisible lint from his black half-zip sweater. He pulled at the collar of his button-down white shirt. "Happy holidays. I came to see you. I know this is a big surprise."

Vikki took a step back. "Pfft! Are you kidding?" She made to turn away, not about to entertain whatever sick joke or trick he had up his sleeves, all the heartache and headache she'd endured over the years because of this man.

"I ran into Ted and Gomez. I couldn't help overhearing what they were saying and why you were in New York. I decided to come up right away."

Vikki was stunned. She and Sean McClane had had beef since her rookie days when Bruce, her fiancé, was alive. One night while meeting up with her friends in a bar, McClane had accosted and groped her as she'd returned from the bathroom. Vikki, a victim of abuse, had fought back. She'd kneed him with all she had in his crown jewels, sending him to the emergency room.

"I think you wasted your time coming here. I have nothing to say to you."

"I can help."

Vikki chuckled. "Help me?" She backed away. "Whatever you're selling, I don't want it."

"Wait, Vikki! I have information you need to know. Hear me out first, please."

The sound of his pleading voice made her stop. Her eyes narrowed. "What type of information?"

He came closer. "I was an asshole then."

Vikki chuckled. "Damn right. Your words, not mine."

"I got what I deserved, but you saved my life."

Vikki raised both hands while shaking her head. "Wow, wow, wow. Back up a little. Saved your life? I made you miserable." Was he trying to butter her up for an end-of-year trick? "You gave as good as you got too."

A flush crept up McClane's neck.

He glanced at his shoes. "After all these years, it's still embarrassing." He paused for a moment. "After you kneed me and...crushed my testicle, I had an emergency orchiectomy—removal of the testicle."

Vikki's eyes widened. Her hands flew to her mouth, cutting off a gasp. "Oh my God, I'm so sorry." Her words were barely audible. So that explained the extended hospital stay and secrecy around why he hadn't returned to work right away. The guys were always tittering around McClane; they knew. Vikki felt terrible. She'd packed all the frustration she'd felt when abused as a little girl by people in authority into that knee.

McClane waved his hand in dismissal. "I'm not done." He drew in a deep breath and exhaled. "A few days after surgery, the histology report came back—an aggressive form of testicular cancer was lurking. It was like a time capsule waiting for the right time to pop out. With its extraction, you inadvertently saved my life. I don't think I'd have willingly gone to see a doctor. It would have been too late by the time I showed up."

Vikki was relieved the whole ordeal had been positive for him, but that was too much information. But why now? "McClane, you taunted me mercilessly for years, even though I saved your life, as you say." She made air quotes.

"It was my ego."

"So, what's your ego telling you this time?"

McClane watched Vikki through sorrowful eyes. "I was there that night."

A chill went through Vikki like an ice cube sliding down her back. She didn't have to ask which night.

"I was the first on the scene after a neighbor reported hearing gunshots. Lloyd arrived after me. Multiple units are usually dispatched. He asked me to secure the back of the house while he took care of the front. I secured the back, and he wasn't there when I returned to the front."

Vikki's eyes were focused on McClane. Her breathing, periodic and deep, with long exhales. "Where was he?"

"I scanned the yard and waited for about five minutes, hesitant to call his cell as it could compromise him if there were an active shooter. Finally, the front door opened, and Lloyd emerged, signaling it was safe. Levin arrived shortly after, accompanied by—"

"Our Captain Levin?" Vikki knew he'd been on the scene but didn't know he was one of the first to arrive.

McClane nodded. "Then, the cavalry showed up. More police officers, CSU investigators, medical examiners—the whole nine yards. After the preliminary crime scene investigation, when Lloyd was driving away, I noticed someone in the back of his car."

"What do you mean?"

"This is all speculation because it was never mentioned,

and I didn't ask. Either he came with the person knowingly, or the person got into his cruiser while we were there."

Vikki's pulse raced. "Who? Edward Poole?"

McClane shook his head. "I don't know. I only remember that incident after I overheard Gomez and Ted discussing you taking off to New York."

Vikki swallowed. Things had just got complicated.

CHAPTER SIXTEEN

Despite McClane's newfound love for her, Vikki struggled to accept his dinner invitation.

"In that case, I'll be heading back to Jersey," McClane said. "What are you going to do?"

Vikki didn't know. It could be a trick from McClane. They said their goodbyes and McLane left.

Vikki got to her hotel room by seven p.m. She sat on her bed, thinking about her day. The visit to the prison with Benson and meeting Poole. She'd caught Poole in a lie. Then there was McClane—showing up like Santa after Christmas.

She recalled her history with him. He'd grabbed her ass and forced his lips onto hers—before she'd kneed him. That wasn't his first rodeo. Maybe he had a history of abusing women. Had he crossed paths with Alexis after she'd left the bar ten years ago? He forced his way into the house, things got out of hand, and he'd shot Mike and strangled Alexis to keep things quiet.

Thinking of the murder weapon...nothing was mentioned about looking at ballistics again. Vikki's mind drifted back to the scenario she was building for McClane.

McClane was first on the scene, then his buddy, Lloyd, arrived. He told him the situation, and they worked together to 'fix' it. The missing minutes McClane claimed Lloyd was missing was when he went in to stage the crime scene. Perhaps remove the video recorder?"

What was McClane's motive for coming to New York tonight? To throw her off? Or cover his ass since she was closing in? When push came to shove, self-preservation always took precedence. She'd also wanted to take a deep dive at Ringo, the barman. But, with new insights coming in, his story sounded authentic.

Vikki's stomach rumbled, reminding her she hadn't eaten anything since breakfast. She called room service and ordered spaghetti with meat sauce.

"How long?" Vikki asked.

The reply was twenty minutes. That was enough time for her to get to the bathroom, wash the prison stench off, and dress up. But one thing was at the back of her mind: Captain Miller Lloyd's name always came up. He was at the center of this shitstorm. She needed answers. But what was she going to do? Call him and say what? She could go back to Jersey and come back after the first of January as planned.

She emptied her coat pocket, and a business card caught her eye. It was Detective Benson's. A plan was taking shape in her mind. Vikki picked up her phone, checked the time, and dialed his number.

CHAPTER SEVENTEEN

"Detective Mattsen! This is a pleasant surprise."

Vikki was amazed by his excitement.

"You changed your mind?"

"No, you said to call if I needed help. I need some information."

Vikki finished the call, showered, and was on the road by eight-thirty p.m. She wouldn't wait until the new year to talk to Captain Lloyd or get closure. She needed to hear what Lloyd had to say. Maybe he hadn't pulled the trigger himself, but he knew something.

Vikki parked next to the mailbox with the number eighteen printed on it. A grand mansion loomed at the end of the cul-de-sac, its pristine white façade dusted with snow. "Wow."

She removed her phone from the dash magnet and rechecked Detective Benson's text with the address. She was at the right place. That was a lot of house on a police captain's salary. But that wasn't her concern for now.

Vikki walked up the driveway. Her feet crunched on the snow, and the crisp air nipped at her. Her breath shot out in front of her with each exhale like a puff from an inhaler. The streetlights threw shadows from the trees on the snow-covered lawn. Snow on the hedge of evergreen shrubs resembled powdered sugar.

The smell of pine, smoke from wood-burning fireplaces, and the cold air reminded Vikki of her childhood and fun Christmases that only lived in her memories. As she approached the front door, the opulence of Captain Lloyd's home awed her. Was it purchased with ill-gotten funds by a man ready to turn the other way if the right amount of money changed hands?

Vikki rang the bell.

Heavy footsteps approached from inside the house. The door opened, and she was taken aback. The captain stood there in a dark sweater and corduroy pants. It wasn't the type of home where the owner answered the door.

"Captain Lloyd," Vikki blurted. "I-I thought I'd drop by and—"

"Detective." He rubbed his hands together. "It's cold outside, and I have only a sweater on." He backed away. "Come in and shut the door."

Had he known she was coming?

Vikki's bravado evaporated in his presence. "Sorry for interrupting your evening."

She glanced around and fell in step behind him. The furniture and decor were antiques mixed with modern, and everything seemed expensive.

"I was expecting you."

Vikki paused.

Captain Lloyd glanced over his shoulder. "Don't be surprised. Detective Benson called me. He works for me, not for you. Remember?"

Vikki swallowed. That was a scenario she'd never played in her mind. She should have known better—the words, rank, and file. Obeying orders meant a lot to her but more to an ex-soldier.

Captain Lloyd cut across the living room, and Vikki followed. A Christmas tree, easily eight feet tall, was at the end of the room. They passed framed pictures of Captain Lloyd and his wife on the wood-paneled wall. And some with a younger couple and their child.

They entered another room that Vikki took for his study. It was furnished in the same style as the rest of the living room, with dark wood-paneled walls and shelves lined with hardcover books. An executive mahogany desk with leather swivel chairs on each side was at the center.

"Please take a seat," Captain Lloyd said. He lowered himself into one and pointed at the other across the table.

Vikki pulled out the chair and glanced around as she sat. The room was nicely done. Even a door behind her blended with the wood-paneled walls. It must lead to the bathroom, she thought. There were more paintings and pictures. A large photo of Captain Lloyd and his family hung on the mantel above the fireplace. She'd seen so much of his family that they now seemed like people she'd met before. He either had a married son or daughter and a grandchild. The family must mean a lot to him.

"Can I get you a drink?"

Vikki shook her head. "Thank you." Her mind raced. She'd come to accuse a high-ranking police officer in his own home of spearheading a cover-up. Where should she start?

"So, how can I help you?"

Vikki took a deep breath and exhaled through her mouth. "I found out this evening that you were one of the first on the scene at my house ten years ago. You entered the house...and—"

Captain Lloyd raised his hand. "Hold that thought. I want

to tell you something that happened earlier, maybe fifteen years ago, when I was a year or two out of the academy."

Vikki wanted to get it all out before she lost momentum but stopped. An unexpected release of tension left her shoulders.

Captain Lloyd began. "I'd responded to a case of drowning at the trailer park in Syosset. When I got there, I recognized the woman and her child. I'd come to the trailer before. The woman and her husband were known addicts. The woman and little girl always had bruises, and the girl had a distant stare in her eyes. A pattern of abuse was obvious. I called it in."

Vikki's insides tightened. The comfortable leather chair she was sitting on felt like concrete. She knew of a similar story. The memories flooded back. Her mouth went dry. She'd worked hard to forget this part of her life, to move on and start anew, but now it all seemed to come crashing back.

Captain Lloyd continued. "I got the report from the woman and her child. CSU investigated, and the ME fished the man out of the tub. A few days later, the autopsy report was returned. The victim had high levels of benzos in his blood. In the cause of my investigation, I discovered that the woman had a prescription of the same medication from her physician to help with sleep."

Vikki was not breathing. She didn't want to give herself away.

Captain Lloyd paused and stroked his chin. "That toxicology report never made it into the report. The case was closed as accidental drowning."

Vikki remembered her mother grinding the pills into powder. Her father had returned from work, and she'd put the powder in his drink. He'd drunk while soaking in the tub and fell asleep. She remembered her tearful mother telling the police she was making dinner, and when she went to tell him dinner was ready, he was underwater. His death was ruled accidental.

Earlier, her mother had told her about little white lies. So when the police came, Little Victoria corroborated her mother's story.

After her father's death, everything had been normal for a while. Even her mother's taste for drugs was met. Without her father drinking, then pissing off the money, the life insurance money went a long way for Vikki and her mother. Eventually, the money ran out, but her mother's drug habits did not. She married her dealer, but he needed to be paid. Victoria knew how her mother had handled that.

The mention of her name drew her out of her reverie. She refocused on Captain Lloyd.

"Detective Mattsen, I'm sorry for what happened to your family, but the case was solved a few weeks ago. An inmate at Nassau owned up to it."

Vikki inhaled and exhaled. The ball had come back to her. "I was at Nassau jail this afternoon, and Poole couldn't recall the statue in the foyer of my house. It was too large to be missed. He was never there. Someone put him up to it."

Captain Lloyd looked like a cartoon character with a glowing bulb hanging over his head. He thought for a moment. "The Venus." It was more of a statement than a question.

Vikki was surprised he'd owned up to it. Now she knew why the captain had taken her back to an event fifteen years ago—quid pro quo. I scratched your back, and now you scratch mine. Forget about this case. I saved your mother many years ago.

"It was a tragedy, a mistake," the captain said. "Nothing can bring them back. Someone has confessed to it. Let it go?"

Vikki ignored what he'd said. But it wasn't lost on her that he still felt in control, like he had an ace up his sleeve. "Mike

Devoe had a video camera facing the entrance and other parts of the house. It must have captured whoever committed those murders, but it was never mentioned in the case file."

Captain Lloyd leveled his gaze at her.

Vikki did not back down. "All I want is the truth. You were the first to enter the house. I can only conclude that you took the video. Who are you trying to protect?"

"Detective, the case is closed. A killer is in jail. Opening up old wounds will never help anyone."

"It is my wound, Captain. And it never healed."

Captain Lloyd leaned back and interlaced his fingers in front of him. A moment passed, then he sat up. He shook his head and said, "I found a video, and when I watched it, I knew it was better for everyone that it never came to light."

Vikki's heartbeat sounded like a bird caught in a hunter's net trying to escape. Her nostrils flared. "The person in that video was responsible for the death of my family. Who was it?"

Captain Lloyd leaned forward, his face red with anger. "You think you can handle the truth?" He stabbed a finger repeatedly in front of her. "*You* were in the video."

CHAPTER EIGHTEEN

Vikki's face crunched up as if she'd bitten into a lime. "What are you talking about?"

"I should have destroyed the tape," Captain Lloyd said. "I was afraid a day like this might come, and here we are."

Vikki placed a hand on her chest. "Are you saying that I, Victoria Mattsen, murdered my own family, and now I'm trying to find the murderer?"

The more the captain spoke, the more incredible his remark sounded to Vikki.

"I didn't murder anyone. All I want is justice—to see the perpetrator pay for their crime. The death of two wonderful people must not be in vain."

Captain Lloyd sighed. He picked up a remote control from the table. "After ten years, we are back to square one." He pointed the remote at a framed watercolor image of lilies. "You'll see for yourself."

The frame was a flat-screen TV. The flowers vanished, replaced by a black-and-white image of the inside of the Devoes' house, the foyer.

Vikki gasped.

She leaned closer. It was like she'd traveled back in time. There was no audio. The man in the leprechaun costume was there in their foyer, receiving people right beside the statue of Venus. The camera then cuts to a group of men sitting and talking around a table. Vikki's eyes narrowed. Where was that?

Captain Lloyd pointed the remote at the TV again. "I'll fast-forward it."

The images moved faster. When Vikki appeared, he stopped it. Vikki's heart was thumping. She was so young. The video jumped again to a group of men sitting around a table. She saw Mike Devoe smiling, shaking hands with the men as they dispersed.

Vikki recognized the location, Mike's study.

The hairs at the back of her neck rose.

Her insides tightened. Her scalp felt like a hundred crawling insects had landed on it. Then they crawled to her armpits.

She resisted the urge to scratch.

Heat crisscrossed her body. Captain Lloyd's library felt like a sauna. Vikki unzipped her coat, desperate for a cool breeze.

She knew what happened next—a memory she'd somehow suppressed. She chewed the inside of her cheek. Mike Devoe had called her to his study. He'd welcomed her back from Paris and was proud of her. He'd said he had something for her and had given her an envelope. Vikki had opened it, read it, and tears flowed down her cheeks. It was his will, and she was a beneficiary.

Vikki shut her eyes. She couldn't watch.

Never had she been so ashamed of herself. She had tried to give herself to Devoe. The only way she thought she could thank him for all he'd done for her.

Mike had been furious and disappointed. She remembered his words—*you're a daughter to me as much as Alexis is*—then he'd stormed out of the room. Vikki had picked up her clothes, dressed, and left the study.

A painful lump formed in Vikki's throat.

She could have told her college friends she couldn't make it to Manhattan, and they'd have understood. What had happened in that video was the real reason she hadn't gone out with Alexis that night. She couldn't face her after what she'd tried to do.

The camera showed Vikki entering the study. Her mouth went dry. She couldn't watch it. Should she walk away? Then Captain Lloyd came to her rescue.

"We don't need to see this. We know what happened." He pointed the remote control at the TV and forwarded the scene.

Vikki exhaled. The long-held breath shuddered out of her.

The camera skipped to when the guests said their good-byes and left. It showed Vikki leaving the house through the main exit. That was when she'd left for Manhattan. The next scene was Alexis leaving the house for the sports bar.

Captain Lloyd forwarded it again and stopped when it showed Alexis returning home. Later, a young man came to the door and rang the bell. Vikki's pulse raced—*don't open the door*. Alexis opened the door, and he pushed her in. Vikki's heartbeat was pounding. Nobody was on camera, but in her mind's eye, she saw what was happening. He'd strangled Alexis and shot her dad. Later, it showed the young man running out of the house.

Vikki committed the face to memory. She'd recognize it the next time she saw it.

Captain Lloyd forwarded the video. He stopped when the front door opened, and a younger version of him entered the scene, gun in hand. He looked at Vikki. "The young man in the picture came to me that night. He'd interacted with Ms. Devoe at the sports bar, and she'd rejected his advances. Later, when he saw her leave, he followed her. The exuberance of youth leads to poor judgment. Add alcohol or drugs to it, and it becomes a keg of gunpowder waiting for a spark."

"Who is he?" Why did you protect him?"

Captain Lloyd raised his hand in a 'wait, I'm not done yet' gesture. "He entered the house, and everything went wrong. Now you see why the tape had to be confiscated," he said. His voice pinched. He locked eyes with her. "We all make mistakes."

Vikki was trembling. "But we all live in a society of laws and order." Her voice was shaky. "The law might not be perfect, but neither is playing God, determining who gets prosecuted and who doesn't. I took an oath to serve and to protect. Follow the law's letter and let the chips fall where they may." Vikki paused. "And I owe Alexis and Mike."

Captain Lloyd sprang to his feet. "Revenge? I protected you and your mother. Because of me, your mother did not face a jury of her peers! She'd have been charged with murder one." He paused. "And what would have become of you? A ward of the state bounced from one home to the next."

Vikki stood. "I'm ashamed of my actions in that video. It can be chucked up to the recklessness of youth and naivete. Morally bankrupt, maybe. But I did not break any laws."

Captain Lloyd's chest rose and fell like he'd run a marathon. His face had turned bright red. An engorged vein appeared on his forehead.

Vikki tapped her chest with her open palm. "Maybe you had good intentions, but because of your tendency to hide information and play God, you did more damage than good."

Captain Lloyd's eyes narrowed. "What...what do you mean?" His voice was low. "I was protecting you. The best place for a child is to be with her mother."

Vikki exhaled. "My mother was hooked on drugs. She married her drug dealer. In place of payment, I was handed to him with smiles and kisses. You succeeded in putting me on a merry-go-round—tossed from one pedophile to another."

Captain Lloyd's mouth dropped open. He blinked rapidly. A guttural sound escaped his throat. He picked up the remote, pointed it at the TV, and the image disappeared in a snap of static.

The room went silent. Their only companions were a ticking clock and the heating furnace's hum somewhere in the house's bowels.

Vikki raised her hand, then let it drop by her side. She took a deep breath and sighed. Shaking her head, she said, "The perp in that video must face the due process."

What happened next made Vikki's inside turn to liquid ice.

"I told you she wasn't going to see the wisdom of letting sleeping dogs lie," a voice said behind Vikki.

Vikki whirled. Her eyes widened. The door in the wall behind her was now open. A figure stood there, pointing a gun at her.

She knew that face. "You!"

"Detective Mattsen, this is your last New Year's Eve."

CHAPTER NINETEEN

Vikki's heart slammed against her ribcage. She recognized the man standing before her, wearing a blue sweater and black jeans.

"John?"

Taylor's husband and Samantha's father. Why was he here and holding a gun? She remembered what the little girl, Samantha, had said yesterday. *My grandpa carries a gun too.* Everything made sense now—no wonder the face in the pictures had been so familiar.

"Lloyd is your father?"

John chuckled. "I thought you'd already figured it out when I tailed you here. I followed you from your hotel." His face got serious like a dark curtain had descended across it.

"You should have left good enough alone. Imagine my shock yesterday when Taylor introduced you. I thought the whole incident was in my rearview mirror. This video coming out is going to destroy many lives. The court of public opinion won't be happy with what you tried to do with your father, Dr. Devoe." He emphasized *father*. "Especially after they learn you also inherited the Devoe fortune."

Vikki's chest rose and fell as she tried to control the rage building inside her. She lost. "You will be locked away in a cell like the animal you are." Her voice was packed with scorn and venom.

John walked over. "Careful now. I'm the one with the gun and have you covered."

"Your ten years of freedom are about to come to an end. You can't get away with this."

"Sure I can. Number one, I was never here. I was at Times Square with my family, watching the ball drop. The story is that you lost your marbles. You drove all the way from Jersey to reopen a case. You went to your old home and harassed the neighbors, threatening them with a gun—demanding information. Scared for their lives, they called nine-one-one."

Vikki shot him a look. "That never happened."

John shrugged. "It doesn't have to happen. We'll say it did, and the policeman on the scene will collaborate. You went to the police station, and they told you the case was closed. Someone had confessed." John shook his head. "You didn't want to believe them because it wasn't the type of punishment you had planned for whoever did it. The prisoner gave you a detailed account."

Vikki watched him like a hawk, biding her time.

"Still not satisfied, you visited Captain Lloyd in his home. He tried to talk sense into you, but you attacked him. Luckily, he shot you first."

"Nobody is going to shoot anybody," said a voice from the entrance to the study.

Vikki couldn't believe her eyes. He was supposed to be back in Jersey. His gun was leveled at John Lloyd.

John glanced at him and returned his gaze to Vikki. "Who the fuck are you?"

"My God, Sean!" Captain Lloyd exclaimed. "What are you

doing here?" The surprise and shock in his voice were unmistakable.

McClane chuckled. "I was crawling around the neighborhood and thought I'd drop in. I can see I came right on time. Okay, we're done with pleasantries. Miller, it's time we stopped lying and put this behind us. John, put down the gun. Miller, tell your boy to put the gun down."

"Dad, who's this clown?"

"The first officer on the scene ten years ago," Captain Lloyd said. "McClane, I thought you'd have said something over the years."

"I should have back then," McClane said. "It's better late than never. I put two and two together after I heard what Mattsen was up to in New York from her partner. Anyway, I met Detective Mattsen earlier at her hotel. I noticed she had a tail when she left, and I followed. Good thing you guys are not big on locking doors around here. My phone is recording both video and audio. A lot has already been—"

John glanced at McClane. "What? You stupid old man!"

Vikki's eyes were on John. She took a step forward.

John's eyes returned to her.

Captain Lloyd sighed. "Oh Jesus, you recorded this?"

"Yes, I understand you were protecting your son, but if we continue like this, we'll end up in a lawless country. Especially with the way things are going."

Lloyd sighed. "Johnny, put down the gun."

"Dad, I'm not going to jail. You promised me."

"I know, son, but a man has to take responsibility for his actions." Lloyd walked toward his son. He stretched out his hand. "Give me the gun."

John shook his head. "I'm not going to jail." He turned the gun away from Vikki to his father and pulled the trigger.

CHAPTER TWENTY

Captain Lloyd grabbed his stomach and went down.

That was all the distraction Vikki needed. She reached for her Glock.

John pointed the gun at McClane and released another shot.

McClane clutched his side, eyes widening. His gun clattered on the floor. He began a slow descent down.

Vikki's gun came free.

But John's gun was already on her—he pulled the trigger.

Vikki flinched. Dodging a bullet only worked in the movies. The bullet slammed into her, pushing her back. Pain exploded in her left shoulder like she'd been jabbed with a burning stick.

John fired again.

Vikki was out of luck. The second bullet hit her in the thigh. Pain washed through her. As he leveled his gun at her, Vikki's leg gave way. She went down. Her claws dug into the butt of her weapon. She held on. Letting go was like throwing in the towel.

"Jesus, Johnny," Captain Lloyd said in a raspy voice. "You shot them."

John went to his father. "I-I had to. I'm sorry I shot you. It seemed like you saw things her way. We'll cover it up, like the last time. Right?"

"Johnny...you're mad," Captain Lloyd said. "Call an ambulance."

"What...what are you saying, Dad?"

"C-call an ambulance," Captain Lloyd repeated.

"What're we going to tell them?" John said.

Vikki used the distraction to her advantage. She sat up, teeth clenched as pain ravished her. Her left hand was limp beside her. She lifted her gun with shaky hands and leveled the muzzle at John's center mass. Her finger was on the trigger, and she was aiming to kill. She'd shoot him in the back if she had to.

John glanced up, and his eyes widened. "Fuck!"

Vikki summoned her energy reserves. "Drop it! Or I drop you!" She was singing to the choir.

John raised his gun.

Vikki tapped the trigger twice.

John flew back. He squeezed out a shot. It went wide.

The shots rang in Vikki's ears. She trailed John with a shaky hand, ready to pump more bullets into him. He'd landed on his back. Two red dots on his blue sweater spread. His mouth opened and closed like a baby bird expecting food from its mother.

Vikki took stock. Captain Lloyd and McClane were on the floor, moaning. She gulped in the air, smelling blood and gunpowder. It brought back memories of the first and last time she and Alexis had gone hunting with her dad.

She glanced at John Lloyd. His mouth remained open, eyes fixed. Vikki placed her gun on her leg and pulled her cell phone from her jacket pocket. She dialed 911. Her hands were sticky, her pants wet, and she was beginning to feel cold.

"Three officers down, one civilian down," she gasped. "We need medical assistance, now."

The dispatcher was asking questions—are you a cop? Location, street number, stay with me. Her hearing faded in and out. Vikki couldn't focus. She was on a boat, drifting away. So, this was what it felt like when people were dying. Her phone dropped from her hand. She lowered her head, and then everything went dark.

CHAPTER TWENTY-ONE

Vikki blinked.

Everything was foggy. A dark oblong face surrounded by a halo loomed over her. She'd died and was at the pearly gates? There must be a mistake. She should be in Hades.

"Vikki? Vikki? Are you awake?" a familiar voice said.

That was her partner's voice, the ME's voice. She must be on his autopsy table. He'd cut her open and released her soul.

"Vikki? It's me, Ted." His voice was desperate.

Vikki blinked some more, and the fogginess fell away. Ted's face emerged. Behind him was a lamp. No halo.

"I'm still alive?" Her words came out as a croak. Her throat was dry. "Where am I?"

Ted's lips parted in a big smile. "Thank goodness. You had me worried."

Vikki tried to move. She winced. "Where am I?"

"Winthrop University Hospital, in Mineola. You finally got yourself shot. You took one on the left clavicle and the other on the thigh. The bullet in the thigh went clean through and missed the important stuff." He gave a thumbs-up. "You'll survive."

"What day is it?"

"January first," Ted said. He glanced at his phone. "It's now seven forty-five a.m. This is what I call starting the new year with a bang. You were brought in from Lloyd's place just before midnight."

Vikki shut her eyes, remembering the moment she was shot. She swallowed. "My throat is dry."

Ted picked up a cup of ice and water with a straw and put it close to her lips. "Here."

Vikki sucked on the straw. The water cooled everything in its path as it traveled down. She drank half of the cup. That was good. "What about McClane...Lloyd?"

"McClane sent me a text after he saw you. I started coming to usher in the new year with you."

Vikki smiled. "I'd planned the same thing until I met McClane at the lobby of my hotel and changed mine."

There was a knock. The door opened, and a nurse walked in.

"Hello, I'm Nurse Adriana. Ah, you're awake. How do you feel?"

Vikki nodded.

The nurse picked up Vikki's chart from the foot of the bed and scanned it. "Looks good. Is it okay to take your vitals and examine the dressing?"

"Yes," Vikki said.

"How's the pain?" Nurse Adriana asked. She strolled over to Vikki and clipped an oximeter on Vikki's finger.

Vikki made a face and shook her head.

"So-so," the nurse said, nodding. "I have something for that. It will make you sleep, so get on with your conversation before the curtain comes down. Sleep helps with healing." She removed the oximeter and wrapped the blood pressure cuff around her arm.

The nurse finished with the sphygmomanometer and told

them the result. She added medication to the IV bag. "That's it for now. I'll be at the nurses' station if you need me."

"Thank you," Ted said.

Vikki thanked her, then turned to Ted.

"John Lloyd murdered Alexis and her dad. I shot him after he shot at me." Vikki exhaled. "He shot McClane and his dad. Can you imagine?"

Ted nodded. "McClane is doing well. He's out of surgery. Captain Lloyd is expected to survive. Both were struck in the stomach." He shook his head. "Unfortunately, John Lloyd didn't make it."

Vikki shut her eyes. An image of little Samantha and her mother flashed through her mind. She'd made her mother a widow. Vikki's vision got cloudy, but she had no choice. "I've left the girl without a father."

"It was a kill-or-be-killed situation," Ted said. "You did the right thing."

Vikki shut her eyes. A tear trickled down her face into her ear.

Ted wiped it off. "Gomez called earlier. He's on his way. With you out of commish, he won't be retiring soon."

Vikki smiled. She wanted to say that perhaps she should retire with him, but she was too tired. The words only remained as thoughts in her mind. Within seconds, she was fast asleep.

A week after Vikki had been shot, Nurse Adriana took her in a wheelchair to see McClane. He'd undergone three surgeries and had part of his intestines removed.

"It's better than dying," McClane said. "Especially after surviving cancer more than seven years ago. If it wasn't for you, I wouldn't be here."

Vikki laughed. "All's well that ends well." She glanced around his hospital room. There were a few get-well cards and one flower in a vase. Vikki had a ton of cards and flowers in her room. She hadn't known she was that popular. She had enough flowers to start a flower shop, she'd told Ted.

"You seem all mended," McClane said.

"I'll be heading back to St. Ives today. I can't wait to work with you in a more friendly fashion in the office when you return."

McClane pursed his lips. He didn't say anything for a moment.

"Are you okay?"

"I don't think I'll be coming back. I'll take early retirement. The doctors said I'd be fine with a few diet changes. I'll dust off my bucket list and start working through it." He inhaled and exhaled. "The surgeon said the bullet narrowly missed my abdominal aorta. I'd be singing—angel, angel, here I come. Life is too short, and this is my second lease on life."

Before Vikki could respond, there was a knock on the door. She raised her eyebrows in a 'should I get it?' gesture. He nodded.

"Yes, come in."

The door opened, and Captain Levin strode in. He had two bouquets with him. He looked like a shy parishioner walking up the aisle to hand the communion to the priest. He stopped in his tracks.

"I think I just saw a unicorn," Captain Levin said. "We should take a picture—McClane and Mattsen in the same room with no one bleeding. This is a rarity!"

McClane smiled sheepishly.

"How are you, Vikki?" Captain Levin asked.

Vikki was about to jump to her feet, but her thigh wasn't entirely out of the woods. "Doing a lot better, thank you."

"Good thing you are here," Levin said. "Two for one. I was going to drop by your room, too." He handed her one of the bouquets. "From SIPD. They wish you guys a speedy recovery."

Almost all of them had been here to offer moral support and congratulation for flushing out the killer. Because of the cover-up, most people did not dwell on how and what had happened.

Levin turned to Sean. "I heard you'll be out of here in no time."

"Vikki's ready to get back to work," McClane said. "I still have some distance to cover. I was telling Vikki that as things are, I might—"

Another knock interrupted McClane. The door opened, and Ted entered.

"Hey, my favorite pathologist," Captain Levin said.

McClane smiled. "Ha, wait until Dr. Patel hears that."

Then the room went quiet as if a ghost had passed. Dr. Patel had been the ME for the St. Ives police department for a long time. He'd returned to the country of his youth, as he put it, after being diagnosed with end-stage pancreatic cancer. His abrupt departure was how Ted got the job.

"Detective McClane is trying to humor us," Ted said. He came over and kissed Vikki on the cheek. "When I went to your room, and it was empty, I thought you couldn't wait anymore and left on your own."

Vikki chuckled. "No way."

"McClane, I'm glad you're doing great," Captain Levin said. He brushed off invisible lint from his navy-blue winter coat. "I have to go. I have an appointment with Ashton's interim police chief. Get better soon." He pointed to Vikki. "Take all the time you need. I'll see you in St. Ives." He headed for the door.

Vikki turned to McClane. "I have to go." She got off the wheelchair and hobbled with her cane over to him. She leaned over and kissed him on the cheek. "Take care, and thanks. See you when you get back."

"Thank you," McClane said.

Ted brought the chair closer to the bed, and Vikki sat. He wheeled her to the door.

McClane spoke again. "I hope you found closure with your family."

Vikki glanced over her shoulder. "Justice was served."

"Sometimes I wonder what made Lloyd do what he did. What makes us as humans do stupid, life-changing things? For me, I was a coward."

Vikki knew the answer to that. "Love—love for self and family. He wanted to protect his son."

"Yes," McClane said. "Lloyd confessed to me. He said he'd

returned home, and his son told him what he did. They were on their way to the house when the dispatcher put in the report about gunshots fired. He arrived and told me to check the back while we waited for backup. Once I was out of the way, he went in, wiped down everything his son could have touched, and stole the video disk."

Vikki nodded. "Preservation of people we love and of self —then we live with the decisions we made.

"I guess you're right," McClane said. "See you soon. Bye, Ted."

Vikki's eyes drifted up to Ted, and she smiled. "Let's go, babe." She knew all about self-preservation. Nobody was coming to save you.

Vikki never talked about life with her stepfather and mother. The best-kept secrets were the ones you kept to yourself. The trailer they'd lived in had a faulty gas cooker. They were used to the ever-present odor of propane. A buddy of her stepfather had once commented about it.

"You need to fix it. Or one day, kaboom! Charred meat," the man had said.

Vikki was fascinated when she'd heard that. She'd filed it away.

Vikki's stepfather had convinced her mother that she could have all the drugs she wanted if she'd make payment using her daughter. Her mother had agreed.

Vikki knew that her stepfather always lit a cigarette once he woke from a nap after having his way with her. That day, two years after her mother had drowned Vikki's biological father in the tub, was no exception. With smiles and cajoling, her mother had invited Vikki to her marital bed.

The abuse was almost daily. What sort of mother did that to their child? Her stepfather's behavior was routine. He'd take a deep nap. When he woke up, he'd reach for his smokes.

That day his routine was the same.

He'd awoken and found his cigarette. That had been Vikki's cue to exit the trailer. She'd opened the propane tank and left. When the explosion had happened, she, too, had underestimated the force of the blast. She'd been lifted off her feet and tossed a few meters away before darkness had taken her.

She'd regained consciousness when the emergency personnel arrived at the scene. Her mother's and stepfather's remains, strewn all over the trailer park, were picked up in black plastic bags. Months later, investigators blamed the explosion on the faulty cooker.

Little Victoria had ended up in the hospital, where she'd run into Alexis. The least she could do for the girl with a pure heart who'd saved and changed her life was to avenge her murder.

The End

ABOUT THE AUTHOR

Ifeanyi Esimai is a mystery and crime writer and enjoys reading across different genres. When he's not writing or reading, he's exploring documentaries on museums and ancient history.

Click here or the image to get all ten books!

Get a FREE copy of The Rookie!

Join my reader group for updates, giveaways, teasers, and a FREE copy of the prequel - The Rookie. Click here or scan the QR code

www.ingramcontent.com/pod-product-compliance
Lightning Source LLC
Chambersburg PA
CBHW051503050726
47593CB00005B/2207